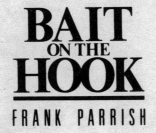

BAIT
ON THE
HOOK

FRANK PARRISH

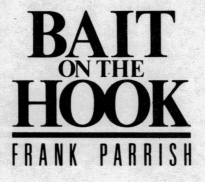

BAIT
ON THE
HOOK

FRANK PARRISH

PERENNIAL LIBRARY
Harper & Row, Publishers
New York, Cambridge, Philadelphia, San Francisco
London, Mexico City, São Paulo, Sydney

A hardcover edition of this book is published by Dodd, Mead & Company, Inc. It is here reprinted by arrangement.

First PERENNIAL LIBRARY edition published 1984.

Library of Congress Cataloging in Publication Data

Parrish, Frank.
  Bait on the hook.
  I. Title.
[PR6066.A713B3 1984]   823'.914   83-48957
ISBN 0-06-080707-5 (pbk.)

84 85 86 87 88 10 9 8 7 6 5 4 3 2 1

1

It was nice to have a midnight invitation to Medwell Old Hall, Dan Mallett thought. It was history repeating itself, with a few differences.

A dozen years before, that earlier time. Dan had recently started at the bank in Milchester, wearing a neat little blue coat and neat little black shoes, polite and punctual, good at figures and good with people. How pleased and proud his mother was, how burning with ambition for him to scurry up the ladder of success, how clearly visualizing the shiny little car, the demure suburban house with clipped privet hedges, a ding-dong door-bell, wall-to-wall carpets . . .

Dan remembered that phase of his life with incredulous horror. But he remembered Sylvia Trenchard with grateful pleasure. She was twenty then, a very little younger than himself. She had lived with her grandparents at the Old Hall since her parents were killed by a drunk driver in 1965. Her father's parents took her in, old Colonel Trenchard and his rubbery wife, and she grew up in that isolated ancient house. She was away a lot, at boarding school and staying with schoolfriends, because there was not much for her to do at the Old Hall, with the old people. She became very pretty (her mother had been a beauty). Dan eyed her with keen interest the few times he saw her. He liked her face, what he could see or guess of her body, and her manner. She was friendly. The old Trenchards were powerful snobs, keeping alive traditions that were dying all round them. But Sylvia was a modern girl. In spite of her expensive education she took people as she found them and made friends where she found them.

She found Dan in her grandfather's garage one night. He was returning the colonel's car, which the colonel did not know he had borrowed. He was not a conventional bank-clerk. She was coming back from a party in her own small car. It was midsummer, breathlessly hot even at three in the morning. She was dressed strikingly, revealingly, for some big party in some big house. He was dressed for a very small party, in old khaki pants and denim shirt. For him it was a thoroughly embarrassing confrontation, with probable consequences of an odious kind.

From an early age, Dan had been made aware of his effect on females. It was not a thing to take pride in, but it was useful, a way of getting out of ugly situations as well as a way of getting into nice ones. Rather despairingly, Dan tried his best smile on the ravishing Miss Trenchard – the disarming little-boy one, which was also intended to convey a gratifying hint of lecherous admiration.

She told him afterwards that the party had been an appalling bore and she was in a mood to do something crazy. It was lucky for him that the crazy thing she chose was taking him to bed with her. She said it was lucky for her, too. Her previous experiences had been messy and frustrating. With him, she said, it was lovely, really lovely for the first time. They repeated the loveliness in the dawn; then Dan dressed, and kissed her, and crept away.

After that they met when they could. It continued to be lovely. There was no deep emotional involvement, but they became friends as well as lovers. They made one another laugh.

To Sylvia, an affair with Dan was partly an expression of rebellion (very secret rebellion) against the ossified rules of her grandparents; it was an assertion of her independence, of being a free adult in a free society; it was an exploration, continually surprising, of a personality unlike any she had ever met, and of a lifestyle (for she came once or twice to the snug but crazy cottage, once a gamekeeper's, under the dripping edge of the Priory Woods) completely outside her experience. It was also fun and physically exciting. She told him all this. She was a very gabby girl.

Then she married the Dutchman.

She told Dan all about that, too, when they met to say good-bye. It was a long good-bye, three lovely hours. Piet

Vandervelde was very handsome and fascinating and cosmopolitan and rich, already at thirty head of the London branch of his family company. He was a pilot, an accomplished pianist. He offered her glamour and far horizons. A whirlwind romance followed: Sylvia swept off her feet; grandparents aghast, then mollified by Piet Vandervelde's charm, wealth, power and perfect English.

The Vanderveldes had a house in London. Dan pictured a glittering life. They came down sometimes, and Sylvia continued to see Dan – innocently, secretly because Piet would not have understood. He had Continental notions.

Dan's father died, of hiding in a wet ditch all night when he was almost caught poaching pheasants. Dan inherited a lurcher, a pointer, a Jack Russell terrier, a shotgun, a number of nets and other machines devised for illegal midnight purposes, and – long dimly realized, long fought against – a passionate hatred of collars and indoors and office routines, a passionate love of the secret world of woods and hedgerows, of independence and solitude and self-sufficiency.

Dan left the bank and, as inevitably as Piet Vandervelde, inherited his father's business. His mother was horribly disappointed, betrayed. Dan felt sorry about that, but not so sorry that he ever dreamed of returning to peonage. He could still, however, when rare occasion demanded, dress like a banker and talk like a banker, and thus operate certain ruses impossible to a poacher dressed as a poacher.

Dan did odd jobs by day, slowly, not wishing to exhaust himself so as to be unfitted for his major nocturnal tasks. He did odd jobs for Colonel Trenchard at the Old Hall, now a widower. With him, as with other nobs, Dan adopted a treacly, antediluvian Wessex voice, derived in part from the novels of Thomas Hardy (he found *Under the Greenwood Tree* the most useful), in part from gross parody of a few elderly local characters. Sylvia saw and heard this charade. It made her laugh so much she nearly gave their past away.

Somebody did give it away. Dan and Sylvia had been discreet, in the months of their frolic, but there was a girl in the village who wanted Dan badly for herself (he had that effect on many girls) and she followed them and spied on them, and kept the secret for a long time; and then, in a moment of bitterness, when Dan turned her down again, wrote the truth to Piet in a letter.

Dan did not see Sylvia for months after that, but there were rumours in the village – a flaming quarrel, shouting, violence; the whole thing too much for the frail old colonel, who had a heart attack and died. Killed by Piet, killed by the jealous girl. Killed by Sylvia, in a sense.

Sylvia inherited the house. By this time she had a baby girl called Anna. She and Anna lived at the Old Hall all the time, with a couple in a cottage looking after them. Piet Vandervelde was there at weekends.

Sylvia was generally liked in the neighbourhood but Piet, in eighteen months, made himself generally detested. He was accomplished and attractive; he was arrogant and heartless, guided by no principle except self-interest. He closed footpaths, cut down loved trees, caused hideous development in beauty-spots, somehow evading legal restraints by means of bribes or influence or threats; when he sold he cheated purchasers, when he bought he cheated vendors. It was said that he knocked Sylvia about, which was why she could not have a second baby.

Dan had a horrible feeling that he was himself a reason for Piet's bashing Sylvia. Maybe *the* reason, the beginning of that barbarity. Sylvia never admitted any of that. She told Dan to stay away from the Old Hall, said that Piet would shoot him if he saw him there: perhaps shoot her too. He was violent. In his rages he was a crazy man. He was fanatically defensive of his property, like many rich men, and Sylvia was his property.

A death in the family firm promoted Piet to some exalted role in Amsterdam. Sylvia refused to go with him. She had had enough. He wanted to take Anna, still only a toddler, but the courts forbade him. He swore he would one day recover his adored child. The courts disagreed, and Sylvia strongly disagreed.

Business often thereafter brought Piet to London. According to gossip in the village, he tried to see Anna and take her with him out of the country. Sylvia hid Anna. Because of the threat of abduction, she had the help and approval of the lawyers. Piet was very angry. Everyone who knew him – everyone in the village – knew he would try again.

Sylvia and Dan remained on cordial terms. They might have resumed their affair, but they never did. Sylvia had to be careful, because of her custody of Anna. She had many admirers, some of whom came to the Old Hall. Dan saw them in the distance, hoping they were kinder than Piet, hoping Sylvia was sensible. One admirer gave her a dog to replace the old spaniel that had been the colonel's.

The dog-giver was the most frequent of Sylvia's visitors. He was called Ralph Watts, a fact which Sylvia falsely supposed was kept secret from the village. He lived in Kent, where his mother and sister bred dogs; he was an estate agent, a little slim man, much of Dan's own build, but very fair. He seemed perfectly all right, to Dan and to the village, except for not having any money. There was speculation, in pub and post office and cottage kitchen, about an affair and about marriage. But it was said that if Sylvia remarried, she lost the substantial income which Piet was obliged to pay her. This did not end speculation about an affair.

The trouble was, according to what the village heard, that Ralph Watts was not just poor but certain to remain so. He was simply no good at making money. This might have been thought to make him undesirable to a lady like Sylvia, who wanted and needed plenty of money, and had got used to it. But the village psychologists saw deeper than that.

'It d'go by contraries, d'ye see,' said Curley Godden in the Chestnut Horse. 'Mrs Van were wed to a bloke were *too* good at maken money, an' she did turn agen 'at sort. What d'she turn to? A-course she d'do turn t'contrary.'

It did make a kind of sense. Sylvia was one for turning to contraries. She had turned to Dan as a contrary.

Meanwhile the dog was a sensible present, a kind thought. The house was isolated and the colonel had left some good things, pictures and silver. The couple were still in the cottage, George and Dorothy Barrow, gardener and cook, but they were getting on. George Barrow would not be much good against a tough with a cosh.

The dog Ralph Watts gave Sylvia was an Irish wolfhound, a magnificent bitch called Sophie, as big as a pony. He got her free because his mother bred wolfhounds: he would never otherwise have been able to afford her. Sophie was gentle and affectionate, adoring little Anna and suffering, with slobbering tolerance, her ears and tail to be pulled. She was a marvellous guard dog: her bark could be heard for miles, and she defended her castle with awesome ferocity. One night a couple of nasty bits of work from Milchester tried to do the Old Hall, with a stolen van and a sack for the silver and a sawn-off shotgun. Sophie mangled them both. She would have killed them if Sylvia had not called her off. Sylvia rang for an ambulance as well as the police, and it was needed. Of course everybody heard about it, and then nobody uninvited went anywhere near the Old Hall. Sylvia, Anna, silver and pictures, were as safe as the Crown jewels.

Little Anna was sent away to school, as a weekly boarder. Dan thought this grotesque at her age, eight or nine, but Sylvia said it was necessary. She said the child needed the company of girls of her own class. She said Anna should be subjected to the judgement of her peers. For Sylvia had become as much of a snob as her grandfather; she had reverted, and was strict with Anna and strict with everybody. She was now pretty strict with Dan, when they met. Dan was amused by the change, but he regretted it. He still thought of Sylvia with grateful affection, but there was now no point in their paths crossing.

It was a bit like his own life in reverse. He had spent a period pretending to be conventional, ambitious, almost completely deluding himself, until the shock of his father's death showed him what he himself really was. Sylvia had spent a period pretending to be unconventional, liberated, almost completely deluding herself, until her grandfather's death, the break-up of her marriage, her thirtieth birthday, Anna growing up, local responsibilities, and owning the house, all combined to show her what she herself really was, and had been all along. It was a funny situation, ironic.

One of the people Sylvia was strict with was the village bobby, PC Gundry. With Anna away at school all week for half the year, Sylvia had time for committees. She joined a great many. One or more leaned on PC Gundry, chasing him for laxity in regard to children bicycling on the pavement in the village street, the slamming of car-doors outside the Chestnut Horse at closing time, the fouling of the churchyard by dogs, and other threats to the quality of life in Medwell Fratrorum. PC Gundry had a hunted look, Dan heard in the pub, whenever Sylvia stopped her car outside the police station, which was a breeze-block extension of his cottage next door to the post office. PC Gundry, goaded into rigorous enforcement of the law, became a pest.

PC Gundry had inherited from his predecessor a virulent hatred of Dan Mallett. It was shared by most policemen, and all gamekeepers. Dan was automatically suspected of everything that happened round Medwell, and quite often arrested. They had never got him to court, but they had come damned near it. Dan's continued freedom to commit further atrocities was gall to PC Gundry. Dan guessed he actually prayed for a fair cop – Dan caught in the act of setting a snare or nicking a candlestick.

Prison would have been disagreeable for Dan, but a disaster for his mother. Her arthritic hip was getting worse. She would never be able to manage on her own for more than a few days, in the cottage with the cramped stairs and the old wood-burning stove, with the cooking and cleaning, the dogs and bantams and pigeons. They would take her away and put her in an institution, and she would die of rage. PC Gundry ignored this aspect of the case, and continued to be obsessed with putting Dan behind bars where he belonged.

The Gundrys had a daughter, a skinny little tow-head they called Julie. Dan liked children, Julie Gundry as much as any, but they didn't become close friends, not when she had a nasty-minded nosey parker for a father. Probably the kid was ordered to stay away from notorious characters like Dan.

Julie went away to some kind of college. No doubt she came home from time to time, but Dan never saw her. Then she came back a qualified children's nurse, and she came back a smasher.

The change was astonishing. She was grown up. She was still slim, but she had bumps where girls were entitled to have them. She had nail-polish and nice clothes. It was impossible to understand how this desirable, superior young lady could have sprung from Jim and Beryl Gundry.

Some of the village said Julie was too big for her boots. Dan thought she was the exact right size.

There was nothing he could do about it. He only saw Julie in the distance. He wasn't going any nearer the police station. He wasn't going within a mile of Jim Gundry, any day he could help it.

Julie had learned an awful lot at college besides diets and ailments. She had previously led a terribly sheltered life – at seventeen at eighteen, there was no question of her being out late, let alone having a latchkey. Being a policeman's daughter, they said, she had to set a good example, just as Dad had to set an example. Boys hadn't come into Julie's life at all. Being a late developer physically made it worse – she looked like a little kid, as well as being treated as one by her Dad.

College changed all that. She filled out and she looked really nice. Also, she got to know girls a lot more sophisticated than she was, experienced girls who had spent whole nights with their boyfriends. They teased her for her ignorance and innocence. They put the ignorance right, and she put the innocence right. It wasn't much fun at first, but she got the hang of it.

Dad would have killed her if he knew. That was half the joy.

For the years of her childhood in Medwell, after they had come to the village and before she had gone away to college, Julie had heard, like a litany over tea at home, the sins of the local villains, the miserable softness of the magistrates, the cunning of the criminals. Dad was truly indignant. That put her on the side of the criminals, because she was almost in prison herself.

The one she really loved was Dan Mallett. Lots of the girls at the village school had crushes on Dan, because of his amazing blue eyes, because he called nobody master, because he was a kind of pirate, a bandit, cocking a snook at the whole country, the whole world, all the boring faces of law and order like Julie's Dad, and getting away with it.

''*Tis my delight on a shining night*' was the favourite song of a lot of the girls at the school. Poaching was romantic. Dan was romantic. There were fights over him, between young girls, about which he preferred and which loved him most. One time Miss had to empty a bucket of water over two girls who were fighting, they were that wild and hysterical.

Julie never got into fights over Dan because she barely knew him. He didn't come up and joke with her, as he did with the others. Julie knew why: it was because her Dad was a bobby. It was unfair, sickening.

Julie came back with her certificates and her medals, knowing she was pretty, knowing she was grown up. She decided at once to stay in Medwell as short a time as possible. She felt stifled in the cottage and stifled by her parents. She was grateful to them, but she wanted to live a different kind of life, maybe abroad, maybe in America.

Meanwhile she took a job with Mrs Vandervelde, the bossy lady at Medwell Old Hall, looking after nine-year-old Anna in the summer holidays. It was a lovely job in some ways, a lovely quiet place, but difficult in others. She didn't live in. She slept at home, except when Mrs Vandervelde was away for a night. Then of course she slept at the Old Hall, feeling quite safe because of the huge dog Sophie. Nobody could come anywhere near the house at night without Sophie hearing, and nobody would dare come in. Mrs Vandervelde could have left all the doors unlocked. Also there was a couple living in the cottage by the house, so Julie was not completely alone with Anna. It would have been another matter without Sophie and without George and Dorothy Barrow in the cottage. It was a dark old house, scary. But Sophie was there and the Barrows were there, so that part of the job was all right. The trouble was that Mrs Vandervelde was tremendously old-fashioned, as strict as a dragon, for all she was not much over thirty; and Anna had just as strong a character as her mother. She was a child you had to be firm with, but you had to understand and explain. Mrs

Vandervelde didn't. She gave out orders and expected Anna to jump. Anna didn't jump. She argued. She dug her toes in. Out came the slipper.

Yet mother and daughter were very close, adored one another. Anna was happy when she was not sulking or in a temper – she did have a temper, her father's apparently. There were stories about that, in the village shop and over the Gundrys' tea-table.

The job ended when Anna went back to school in September. But Mrs Vandervelde asked Julie to come some weekends when Anna was at home. Julie was glad to oblige, until she got a proper full-time job. The money was useful.

That was how things were in October, Julie bored stiff in Medwell, waiting for the agency to find her the job she wanted, feeling stifled when she was at home and aimless when she was out of it.

She saw Dan Mallett in the distance, a time or two. Of course she had outgrown her schoolgirl crush on him. But he was still a romantic bandit, a venturesome loner catching birds and animals in the moonlight under the noses of all the squares. He was still her Dad's pet aversion. He still had those amazing blue eyes.

The third weekend in October, Anna came home from school with a bad cold. Mrs Vandervelde decided to keep her at home on Monday, to give her a chance to shake it off. Julie was called in to help. She was needed to keep a bored and fretful child occupied, while the mother went off on her committees.

Julie was late going home. She rode her bicycle, for there was no car for her to use, and the Old Hall was too far from the village to walk. It was cold, frost in the air. It was very still. Julie's bicycle lamp seemed very feeble in the huge surrounding darkness.

She used the short cut, as she always did, the footpath behind Yewstop Farm. It meant lifting the bicycle over a stile, but that was no problem to a sturdy country girl like Julie. Only somebody was sitting on the stile, a small figure with untidy brown hair, a wedge-shaped face, an old tweed coat, and a very broad sweet smile outshining the beam of the bicycle lamp which illuminated it.

'Who'd ever a-ben an' guessed,' he said, 'that ye were a bluebottle's babby.' His voice sounded to Julie like treacle, slow and sweet.

'Dan Mallett!' said Julie. She felt the breadth of her own answering smile. She added, surprising herself, 'Do you always talk like that?'

'Not invariably,' said Dan, in a quite different voice.

'Why are you sitting in the cold in the dark? Are you poaching?'

'Not at this moment. I've been waiting for you.'

'Oh,' said Julie, delighted and excited and puzzled. 'Why?'

'Acos,' said Dan, treacly and antique again, 'ye're the prattiest thing a-seed yerabouts. But a-bent in the way o' knocken on a bluebottle's door.'

'No, don't do that . . . How did you know I'd come this way?'

'I know almost everything about everything,' said Dan in his other voice, which was like Julie's own new college voice. Reverting, he said, 'A-ben creepen up an' creepen down, wi' me ears a-flappen. A-did b'lieve ye went up to Old Hall, a-cossettin the babby wi' the snivellens. A-did b'lieve ye'd welcome company, t'see ye homeways a night as black as a badger's privy.'

'I do welcome it,' said Julie shamelessly.

He lifted the bicycle over the stile, effortlessly, although he looked too frail to lift a matchbox. He was slim but he was made of wire. He was just the same height as Julie. She made this discovery when he kissed her, which he did almost immediately.

'This is awful,' said Julie, with complete insincerity.

'We're old friends,' said Dan.

They walked along the footpath, their way lit by Julie's bicycle lamp. Dan wheeled the bicycle. Every so often he stopped, leaned the bicycle into the hedge, and kissed her. She responded with cordial enthusiasm. His caresses became, by gentle and reassuring stages, more passionate. There was no doubt what was in his mind. There was not much doubt in Julie's mind, either.

They chatted easily. Julie was a direct, extrovert girl, and Dan was not a person anybody could feel shy with. He made her laugh. Her laughter made him kiss her with a new energy and a new degree of friendly lechery.

'It's too cold,' said Dan, keen regret in his voice.

Julie knew exactly what he meant. All this should have been happening in July, a night as dark but air like velvet.

'I can't take you home,' she said. 'Dad says you're the biggest villain unhung.'

'I can't take you home either,' said Dan. 'There's no empty house I can think of we could borrow. There's shelter to be had, haylofts and such, but no warmth.'

'No time, either,' said Julie. 'Dad's probably already on the phone to Mrs V., asking where I've got to. She'll have told him what time I left.'

'Nasty-minded old nosey,' said Dan. 'Sorry, love. Slipped out. Are you sure he's truly your Dad?'

'Can you imagine my Mam with a travelling salesman?' said Julie.

Dan laughed. He kissed her, his hands busy under her winter coat. She clung to him, feeling fast and wicked and shameless and happy.

He left her at the edge of the village, kissing her good-bye, saying he would make a plan.

She was not very late home. Her mother remarked on her high colour and the brightness of her eyes. She said it was the cold air. Her father said she had a silly grin like an idiot. She had no answer to that.

Dan was frustrated. Julie would be going away soon, to some job maybe on the other side of the world. Then the chance would be gone. But still he could go nowhere near the Gundrys' cottage. With his mother housebound, there was no way he could smuggle Julie into his own tiny bedroom. His mother slept badly and lightly. He would not shock the old lady with anything so blatant as a visible affair, although, to be sure, he knew she knew quite well how he spent some of his time. Anywhere out of doors was out of the question; anywhere under cover was out of the question unless it was heated. It was weather for a bed in a bedroom, maybe a hearthrug in front of a fire, but not for any of the delightful improvisations of midsummer.

He kept an eye out for empty houses, for people going away for weekends. But everyone was perversely fast at home. It was an unusual predicament for him, a thoroughly annoying one. Julie in his arms felt exactly as he had expected, and he wanted her badly.

They snatched moments together, hiding by day or hidden by night. But they were only moments. They were nice, but they gave Dan a tummy-ache. There was not the slightest chance of the old Gundrys going away and leaving Julie alone in the cottage, or of Dan's mother being out for the day or dead-asleep at night.

Julie said hurriedly, 'I've got to spend Saturday night at the Old Hall. Baby-sitting. Mrs V. is going to be away.'

'There's the folk at the cottage,' said Dan. 'Old George Barrow and his woman. Great ones for peering and prying, those two.'

'They're away. They're staying with their daughter in Yeoville.'

'There's that dog, that monstrous hound. She'd tear me in little bits and eat my buttons.'

'*No, no, no!* That's the point. Mrs V. is taking the dog to the breeder in Kent where she came from. To be lined or covered or whatever you call it. Married. It's a champion. It's a good idea, actually, Sophie ought to breed. The people are friends of Mrs V.'s so she's staying the night. She'll be away most of Saturday, and Saturday night, and most of Sunday. So will Sophie. I'll be scared to death in that great gloomy house, all by myself except for Anna.'

'Oh, you ought to have company,' said Dan. 'No doubt about that. Protection. Security.'

'I thought you'd think so,' said Julie, blushing and giggling like a very small girl.

Dan helped his mother upstairs and into bed. She refused a hot drink or an aspirin. She stared at him from the pillow while he put things to rights in her room, her eyes as bright and suspicious as a ferret's in her old face, which – once smooth and berry-brown – was as white as the pillow-case which Dan had washed and given her fresh that evening, as lined as a piece of crumpled tissue-paper.

'Ye wenchen or thieven tonight?' she asked, never resigned, never to be resigned, to the wicked way of life he had chosen.

'Baby setten,' said Dan. 'Act o' mercy.'

He put on a coat and a cap and a muffler; he took a flask and a pencil flash and the ashplant with a lump of lead in the handle. He got out his bicycle, as quietly as possible. The dogs whimpered. He hushed them. A bantam hen gargled sleepily. He pedalled slowly, seeing well enough without lights, knowing every yard of his road, not wishing to be seen, not wishing to be exhausted when he arrived.

The back road skirted unfenced woods which Piet Vandervelde had added to the Old Hall property. It was locally supposed that he planned to develop or otherwise despoil them. Wavering along the road in front of Dan, on foot, was a stumbling uncertain figure. A man, going blindly not because it was dark but because he was drunk. Even from behind, even in the dark, Dan recognized Blinky Bliss, a scruffy old grouch who did a bit of work for the council by way of hedging and ditching. He was called Blinky because of his thick pebble spectacles which always looked too greasy to see through, but with which Blinky's eyesight was sharp enough. In his job he saw almost as much as Dan did, but unlike Dan he blabbed about it. He was an old mixer – he made trouble for sport. He made trouble for free drinks in the Chestnut Horse, too.

Dan had no wish to be seen by Blinky, who would tell

everyone in the pub that Mallett was thieven or poachen by the Old Hall. Jim Gundry would probably buy Blinky a drink, and then maybe do sums in his head about Julie being all alone there. It was lucky Blinky was drunk.

Dan raised himself from the saddle, leaned over the handlebars, and accelerated like an Italian in a pursuit tone. He pumped at the pedals, gathering speed. He went past Blinky like a silent bullet, slowing down only when he was well round a corner. He doubted if Blinky had seen anything at all. Certainly, in the state he was in, he could not have recognized the crouching back of a bicyclist travelling at high speed.

But Dan was, after all, panting and perspiring when he got off his bicycle by the house.

'Anna went to bed early,' whispered Julie. 'Without her supper. Mrs V.'s orders, the last thing she said before she left.'

'Awful,' said Dan. 'Why?'

'I don't know. The usual. Cheek or disobedience or something. She's a handful. Anyway she's fast asleep.'

'Funny,' said Dan, 'I don't feel sleepy at all.'

Julie shut the servants' door through which she had let Dan in. He heard the Yale lock click. No disturbance was possible. It was eleven o'clock. Julie was wearing a woolly dressing-gown over a nightdress. They crept hand in hand through the dark, complicated house. Floorboards creaked. Stairs seemed to groan with disapproval. Half-way up the stairs, Dan undid the sash of Julie's dressing gown, in order to embrace her more cosily. She trembled under his hands. He felt her smile against his mouth.

Her bedroom was warm, with a dim pink glow from an electric fire.

They marvelled at each others' bodies, staring and stroking.

They had only been waiting for ten days, but it seemed the consummation of a century of yearning.

They heard midnight strike.

Julie lay in Dan's arms, her cheek on his shoulder, her hair tickling his chin, one thigh lazily over his thighs. She was purring. Dan stroked her hair, to express the vivid affection he truly felt, the awed gratitude at the joy they had given one another, and at the same time to stop her hair tickling his nostrils and making him sneeze.

There was a crash from downstairs. There was a shot, a big boom, not a pistol but a shotgun. There was a scream, female, maybe a child.

Julie gave a little scream, and clutched Dan convulsively.

Dan prised her arms away, jumped out of bed, put on her dressing-gown, and ran out on to the landing. He ran to the head of the stairs. The lights were blazing in the hall below.

Little Anna, in flannel pyjamas, was staring open-mouthed at a body which lay face upwards in the middle of the hall. A table was upturned near the body; things kept on the table were scattered all over the stone floor of the hall. A hole was blasted in the body's chest.

The face was unmarked. It stared upwards in death. It was a very handsome face, blond, arrogant. It was Piet Vandervelde, come to abduct his child.

2

There was a little scream behind Dan. It was Julie, in her nightdress. She was staring down at the body, at the well-recognized face which stared sightlessly back. Dan took her hand and they went downstairs. Julie ran to Anna, making a wide detour round the body, and hugged her, hiding the child's face, hiding the child's father's body from her. Dan went a little queasily to the body.

It was certainly a shotgun wound, short range, probably large shot. There might have been some kind of brief fight before, to knock the table over and strew the things on it broadcast. The corpse looked a little dishevelled, as well as having a crater in its chest.

The front door was bolted and chained. There were half a dozen other outside doors. The door Dan had used had a Yale lock only, locked on the spring. No bolts, no chain: all you needed was the key. No doubt Piet Vandervelde had kept his key, and Sylvia had not changed the lock.

Vandervelde had disturbed a burglar. It was obvious. It might not be right, but it was obvious.

How had the burglar got in? Turning on more lights, Dan looked at all the downstairs windows and all the outside doors. All the doors had bolts and all the bolts were bolted; all the windows were latched. Still the same door, then, and another key.

Dan did a lot of sums quickly in his head, and came out not at all with an answer but with one crucial question.

He went back to the hall, his bare feet cold on the stone flags. Julie had wrapped Anna in a rug from the sofa, and taken her away from the shambles. She had wrapped herself in an Inverness cape from the back passage where the coats were hung, and

21

had covered the corpse with a mackintosh. Its feet stuck out, stiff and upward-pointing like the feet of a dead bird.

When Julie came back, Dan said, 'Who knew Sylvia and the dog were going to be away tonight?'

'Nobody,' said Julie.

'But they did.'

'But they couldn't. It was a dead secret. Mrs V. away and Sophie away and the Barrows away. Of course she kept it secret.'

'You knew.'

'I didn't tell anybody except you. You knew.'

'I didn't tell anybody at all. Did your Dad know?'

'Yes,' said Julie, 'they both knew. They had to, to explain my coming. They knew not to tell anybody. They knew the house was completely safe, Anna and I were completely safe, as long as people thought Sophie was here.'

'Did the Barrows know?'

'They might. I don't see how. They'd already gone away when the arrangement was made about the dog. I can't see why Mrs V. would have phoned to tell them.'

'No. The breeders knew, the owners of the stud-dog.'

'Yes, of course.'

'Ralph Watts. His mother and sister. Kennelmaids and such. A servant, whoever made up the extra bed for Sylvia, cooked an extra helping for supper . . . I can't see how any of that can help, but I can't see anything else that helps.'

'What happened, Dan?' said Julie. 'Did a burglar do it?'

'Must assume that, first kick-off,' said Dan. 'But how would any burglar know the dog was away?'

'Saw it going away in the car?' suggested Julie.

'Barely possible. Mighty thin. Keeping the house under observation, month after month, just in case the dog did go away? That doesn't sound right to me. Or miraculous coincidence? That doesn't sound right, either.'

Anna came back into the hall, wrapped in the rug like a squaw. Dan looked at her properly for the first time since she was an infant. She was a skinny little thing, not unlike Julie at the same age, probably much like Sylvia at the same age. She had a lot of long fair hair, very pretty hair. She had a strong little chin with a cleft, and wide, guileless blue eyes. Her nose was sharp and her forehead high. There might be something of her father's arrogance in her face. She looked pretty composed.

She said, 'Who's the man under the mac?'

Julie and Dan looked at her blankly.

Dan remembered that Piet had left when Anna was very small, eighteen months or thereabouts. She did not recognize him. Dan supposed Sylvia kept no pictures of the man who had knocked her about and effectively had killed her grandfather. Anna had no idea who the dead man was. She would have to know, but not yet.

Anna said, 'You're Dan Mallett. You're a sort of friend of Mummy's.'

'More an acquaintance,' said Dan.

'I never knew that,' said Julie.

'Used to do odd jobs for the colonel,' said Dan.

'Why did you kill that man?' said Anna.

'I didn't,' said Dan, startled.

'I think you did,' said Anna. 'And I'll say you did. Unless.'

'Unless what?'

'I don't know yet. Why are you wearing Julie's dressing-gown?'

'To keep warm,' said Dan.

'There's a lot I can tell about.'

'Please don't, darling,' said Julie.

'I will, unless.'

'Let's talk about it somewhere else,' said Dan.

They went from the ghastliness of the hall into a small sitting-room which the colonel had used as an office. It was now chintzy and cheerful. The cheerfulness was a mockery.

Dan considered the implications of his situation. They were as bad as could be. There he was, in the house at the time of the murder. Two people knew he was there and one of them saw no harm in saying so. Nobody had seen anybody else. He was suspected of other burglaries. He was suspected of widespread philandering. He was known to own a shotgun, unlicensed, though it was certainly not in this house.

It was not generally known that he had had an affair with Sylvia, that Piet had been told about it, that there was bad blood between himself and Piet. But a competent detective looking for motive would find all about that in no time.

There was a Detective Chief Superintendent, who knew Dan all too well, who was very competent indeed. He looked like a fox, which was no comfort.

It seemed obvious to Dan that Piet had come for Anna, that somebody had told him that Sylvia and the dog and the Barrows were all going to be away.

The same person, or somebody different, had told the burglar too.

It was no coincidence that Piet, and the burglar, and Dan, were all in the house together on a particular Saturday night. It was the only night any of them would have come, the only possible night, an unrepeatable chance for them all. But how could the others have known to come?

If you knew who knew Sylvia was taking her dog away, thought Dan, you knew who the murderer was.

Dan gulped as he realized the flaw in this reasoning: *he* had known Sylvia was taking the dog away. His mind spun with the implications of this: for Julie as well as for himself.

'You've got an alibi,' said Julie suddenly.

'But I can't use it,' said Dan. 'Think what your Dad would say and do. What Sylvia would say and do. Betrayal of trust and that. Your future. Me being the biggest villain unhung.'

Julie swallowed. She said, 'Even so, I couldn't let anything horrible happen to you, for something I know you didn't do.'

'But he did do it,' said Anna.

'You didn't see him,' said Julie.

'I almost did.'

'Why were you wandering about in the middle of the night?'

'I was sleepwalking,' said Anna, immediately and positively.

'Hungry?' suggested Dan.

'I bet that's it,' said Julie. 'No supper. Wait a minute.'

She trotted away, in the direction of the kitchen. Dan thought it peculiar that, with a bloody and unexplained murder a few minutes old, Julie should be intent on pinning a tiny crime on a small girl. She was back again almost at once, and said to Anna, 'That's stealing.'

'It was made for me anyway,' said Anna. 'Mummy never eats cake.'

'It was very wicked and disobedient.'

'If you tell Mummy I had a midnight feast, I'll tell her Dan Mallett was here in your dressing-gown with nothing on underneath it.'

'Hum,' said Dan, arranging the dressing-gown with more decorum. 'If anybody tells anybody about anything, Anna, your Mum's going to know you had a midnight feast. *When* you'd been sent to bed without your supper. Wow! What does she use, a belt or a slipper?'

'My Dad uses a belt,' said Julie reflectively.

'All in all,' said Dan, 'it seems it's best if nobody knows I was here.'

'All the same I shall tell them,' said Anna. 'Unless.'

'I hate that word,' said Dan. 'Implication o' threat.'

'What are you going to do?' said Anna, looking at him sternly.

'Creep away like a rabbit.'

'And just go home to bed?'

'That would be nice.'

'Then you'll be arrested in the morning.'

'It's possible,' Dan agreed.

'Dad would love that,' said Julie.

'It would be better to find out who really did it,' said Anna. 'You must be a sleuth, like that man on television. Of course he's better-looking than you, and much taller, but you must do the best you can. And then you can tell everybody, and prove it, and be a hero.'

'Fine project,' said Dan.

'I can help.'

'That would be kind.'

'I saw the man.'

'*You what?*'

'I sort of saw him.'

'Now,' said Dan controlling himself, speaking gently, being

25

sweetly reasonable, 'now let's be a little clearer than I am at the moment. You were in the kitchen, eating cake.'

'I had to, I was starving. I was too hungry to sleep. It was unfair – I only told Mummy her lipstick made her look like a tart.'

'Do you know what a tart is, Anna?' asked Julie in a terrible voice.

'Yes of course, silly. Jam in a sort of cup made of pastry. Raspberry jam is best. That's what Mummy's lipstick looked like. That's all I said. It was polite, really.'

'We're getting a mite off the point,' said Dan. 'You were in the kitchen. You heard that crash.'

'It was the hall table. Everything's everywhere. Mummy will be livid.'

'Then you heard the bang.'

'I knew it was a gun. It was too loud for a cork.'

'So?'

'So I was frightened of bandits and murderers, and I was frightened of being caught having a midnight feast. But I thought it was *quite wrong* for people to be letting off guns in our house, specially with Mummy away. So I crept along the passage to the hall.'

'That was brave,' said Dan.

'Yes, I know,' said Anna.

'You were in the dark?'

'I know the way. I often come down to the kitchen after Mummy's gone to bed.'

'Did you find the lights on in the hall, or turn them on?'

'I turned them on.'

'That was rash. Suppose the murderer had seen you and shot you?'

'Murderers don't often shoot little girls. It's quite rare, I think. Anyway I heard him running away along the other passage, towards the other door. So then I turned the lights on and saw him.'

'*You really saw him?*'

'I sort of saw him.'

'What did you sort of see?' asked Dan, very gently.

He felt Julie's fingers clutch his own.

Anna was perched on the edge of a big chintzy chair, her hair brilliant in the electric light, her small face solemn, concentrating, trying to remember.

She said slowly, 'He was just turning the corner in the passage, on the way to the side door. So I only just saw him. He was . . .'

There was no sound, none at all. Anna pushed swathes of long fair hair out of her eyes.

She said, 'He was a great big man. He was very fat.'

'Are you sure about that?' said Dan. 'What about thick woolly clothes?'

'He was very fat,' said Anna, with unmistakable certainty. 'He was wearing a tight sweater. Dark blue. Not a Husky or a sheepskin coat or anything.'

Anna made an excellent witness, thought Dan. There could be no doubt that the murderer was tall and fat.

'Trousers? Shoes?' said Dan.

'Dunno. Sort of jeans. Just shoes.'

'Hair?'

'Yes of course. I'd have said if he was bald.'

'I mean,' said Dan carefully, 'did you see the colour?'

'Black. I only saw a bit because of his cap. He had an ordinary kind of cap, like George Barrow wears.'

'You didn't catch a glimpse of his face?'

'He was running away. He might have had a beard.'

'A beard.'

'He might have. I couldn't see. He was going away.'

'You're being very clever and helpful, Anna.'

'Yes, I know.'

'Is there anything else you can remember? Think very, very hard. Anything at all.'

Anna thought very, very hard. They watched her doing so. She screwed up her face in an agony of concentration, closed her eyes, twitched with the effort of thought. Suddenly her face cleared.

'I knew there was something,' she said. 'It ought to make it easy to find him.'

Dan stared at her. Julie's fingers again clutched his.

'He had a big boil on the back of his neck,' said Anna.

'Hum. Can you be sure? At that distance?'

'Yes of course. George Barrow had a boil on the back of his neck in the summer. He made a frightful fuss about it. He said, "It d'feel like a pair o' they pliers, a-grippen me scruff wi' a pinch."' Anna's imitation of George Barrow's accent was excellent. George was one of the vocal models Dan had used for his own yokel performance, and Anna had him to a T.

'So,' said Anna, reverting as smoothly as Dan himself to normal (though her normal was, he knew, of a different order from his own), 'I know exactly what a big boil looks like, and that man had one, and if it's anything like George Barrow's it'll be there for *days*. So you must be a sleuth and find him.'

'I think maybe I must,' said Dan slowly. 'The other way is, for you to tell all this exactly to Julie's Dad. The police'll probably find this bloke quicker than I can.'

'You're cleverer than Julie's Dad. I heard Mr Goldingham in the Chestnut Horse say you ran rings round Jim Gundry.'

'Sauce,' said Julie. 'What were you doing in the Chestnut Horse?'

'Buying crisps,' said Anna. 'Mummy was visiting the police station.'

'One of those days,' said Julie.

'Anyway, I can't tell it all to the police,' said Anna. 'Or Mummy will know I had a midnight feast.'

'That's not so *very* serious,' said Dan.

'It is to me. It's me she beats. So you've got to go into hiding and not be arrested and find the murderer.'

'Very well,' said Dan meekly.

'And take me with you.'

'Oh no. Oh no!'

'Then I'll tell about you and Julie, and I'll tell about you doing the murder. I'll say that man found you with nothing on, with Julie, and you shot him.'

'My God,' said Julie. 'They'll believe her.'

'You wouldn't do that, Anna,' said Dan, appalled.

The small chin was jutting with massive obstinacy. Anna was determined to get her way. Dan was having no part of it. 'It's powerful cold for lurking in ditches,' he said.

'Pooh. I've got lots of warm clothes.'

'You'll get powerful hungry.'

'We can beg, borrow or steal. I can buy things. I'll be in disguise, of course. You've *got* to take me.'

'But why?' wailed Julie.

'Well,' said Anna, 'there is another reason.'

'Oho,' said Dan.

'I've got to run away from school. Or rather, not go back there. As soon as they start again on Monday they'll know, you see . . .'

'What have you done?' said Julie.

'I think it's prettier, much better, but they won't think so . . . It's a big white carving, of a lady, white stone, just to here, you know –' Anna indicated the bottom of her neck and the top of her shoulders, conveying to Dan that she was talking about a portrait bust – 'it's the lady who started the school. She was called Miss Grimthorpe. We call the statue Old Grim. She doesn't *deserve* to have a statue. Or, if she does, she deserves to have a pretty one. So I made it prettier.'

'What with?' said Dan, full of trepidation.

'You squirt it out of a tin.'

'Aerosol?'

'Yes, like fly-killer. It's purple. It's lovely. So I gave Miss Grimthorpe purple hair and purple spectacles, only they came out like black eyes because you can't do a thin line easily with a squirter, and I gave her a purple moustache . . . And then I discovered it's a special squirter. Miss Hartopp, that's the headmistress, is afraid of being mugged. She has this special squirter. It's only colour, but it won't come off, so you can hunt about and catch the mugger. It's indel-indelib-delible, or something.'

'Ah,' said Dan. 'An' you bear the mark of Cain.'

'No, just a bit on my arm.'

Anna bared her forearm. From elbow to wrist there was a large purple stain, visible from a great distance, lurid.

'I tried to be careful, but I made one bish,' said Anna. 'And I scrubbed and scrubbed and it's still there.'

'They'll look at everybody's hands and arms and such,' said Dan, stirred by a comparable memory from his own school-days.

'So you see I can't go back to school. I *won't*. I'll tell like I said, about you and Julie with nothing on, and the man coming, and you shooting the man.'

'What a little devil you are,' said Dan, reluctant admiration in his voice. 'Absolutely ruthless. Think of your poor Mam, worrying into a decline.'

'I have thought, silly. I'll leave her a note, saying I'm going away with a friend and I'm quite all right, and it's only for a little while, and she needn't worry. And then I can always ring up.'

'An' be nabbed.'

'Not in my disguise I'm going to have. Don't you see, you've *got* to have me with you? I'll know that man again if I see him. It's not the same, my telling you about him. I did it very well, as you said, but still it's not the same. *I* saw him, and *of course* I'll know him the minute I see him again.'

'We search the whole country,' said Dan, 'sixty million people, for a man with a boil on his neck.'

'Yes,' said Anna. 'We can start at Land's End and go all the way up to John o' Groats.'

'Hum,' said Dan. 'There's one sensible thing to do, just the one. What we've got to do, now, immediately, no rubbish, is as follows. Dial 999 and get some clever gentlemen here at once. Julie, you say exactly what happened as you saw it, only leaving me out of it. Anna, you say exactly what you saw, only leaving me out of it. I'll nip away on my bike as soon as I've dressed. I'll be gone before the bluebottles come swarming in. You tell them all about the dog and such, Julie, and they can do the work. Find out who knew, who has keys, who has boils.'

'Why did we wait so long before phoning?' said Julie.

'You should say "telephoning",' said Anna. 'Mummy says it's common to say "phone".'

'I am common,' said Julie.

'Yes, but only a bit,' said Anna.

'Shock,' said Dan to Julie. 'You probably swooned.'

'How soppy,' said Anna.

'There's no reason anybody should ever know you were here,' said Julie.

'Not if nobody says so,' said Dan.

He glanced at Anna. She said nothing. She seemed to have acquiesced, to be accepting the inevitable.

'Brave girl,' Dan said to her.

'I know,' said Anna.

'I'll wait till you've dressed before I phone,' said Julie. 'I mean telephone. Just to be safe. But do be quick.'

'I'm going to my room,' said Anna. 'I'm cold.'

'So am I,' said Dan, still barefooted.

Dan went upstairs and dressed. Julie retrieved her dressing-gown, instead of the Inverness cape.

Dan was tying his bootlaces when he saw, between a crack in the window curtains, headlights sweeping up the drive towards the house.

'Gum,' said Dan. 'Go and telephone this minute. Be telephoning when they get here. It'll look better.'

'But how did they get here? Why are they here?'

'Maybe they'll tell you.'

'What about you?'

'I'll wriggle away.'

She kissed him, and ran downstairs, to the telephone in the hall. Dan peeped out of the window. The police car stopped in front of the house. Its headlights blazed on Dan's bicycle.

Dan could easily have hidden the bicycle. It had never occurred to him to bother. He cursed himself. Such a little, easy precaution. But there was no way he could have guessed there was anything to take precautions against.

A detective, dressed up as a detective in a mackintosh and trilby hat, got out of the car and crossed the gravel to the bicycle. He examined the bicycle in the glare of the police car's headlights. He made notes in a little book. He did not touch the bicycle. Dan's fingerprints were all over the bicycle, and no-body else had touched it.

It was a long walk home.

But as long as he got clear, there was no reason they should be looking for him, bicycle or no bicycle. They'd be looking for a man twice his size with a boil on his neck.

Getting out of the Old Hall was no problem. A dozen years before, when he came to see Sylvia in the middle of the night, he left before dawn without setting foot in the ground-floor rooms. There was a bathroom, and a drainpipe, and the roof of a garage. Sylvia used to unlatch the bathroom window, and leave the rest to him.

He ran along the passage, which was half lit by the lamps in the hall. He heard Julie on the telephone; he heard the doorbell stammer.

Seconds later he was on the roof of the garage: then damaging a lavender hedge. He peeped round a corner. His bicycle was still spotlit by headlights. He set off across country.

They took the mackintosh off the body, and a sergeant recognized Piet Vandervelde. They complimented Julie on having touched nothing. They began to take photographs. They telephoned. They did not ask Julie why she had waited so long before telephoning, because they thought she had telephoned. Somebody had, a woman, saying she was speaking from Medwell Old Hall. Julie was puzzled, but thankful for the let-off.

The police promised not to reveal to the child the identity of the corpse. They would leave that to the child's mother, who would be informed of the tragedy first thing in the morning.

Julie made her statement. She told the exact truth, with a single omission. The police knew all about Sophie the dog, because of the previous burglary. They seized, as Dan had seized, on the crucial question: who could have known the dog was away? Told Piet Vandervelde? Told the burglar?

They took it for granted, it seemed to Julie, that a burglar had been surprised by Mr Vandervelde and had shot him.

Julie said that little Anna was quite capable of answering questions, had actually glimpsed the murderer, could describe him quite well. This was very exciting to the Detective Chief Superintendent, who arrived at this point.

Julie went upstairs to fetch Anna.

Dan pondered, as he loped across country.

Somebody had tipped off the police before Julie even called them. Who? Why? Julie might know by now. It was a thing to ask her.

They would identify the bicycle as his, eventually. Then he'd have some questions to answer. They couldn't get him for loitering with intent, if nobody had seen him loitering. They might think he was a witness to something. They might think he was an accomplice. He tried various stories in his mind to account for the bicycle. He'd been trying to get alongside Julie, but had so far failed because of her Dad? No good, unless he had known the dog was away, and how would he have known that? He'd left his bicycle there the day before, having gone with the idea of asking for work at Old Hall, and then been offered a lift back to the village? By whom? A stranger. A stranger unseen by anybody else, a car unseen by anybody else? No good.

He realized he was too tired to think clearly. He would have time to think in the morning, long before the police got around to bothering him. Meanwhile the important thing was Anna's having seen the big fat man with the boil.

It was three in the morning when Dan got home. There was frost in the air and the grass rustled starchily. He hushed the greeting of the dogs. He had a nightcap, Scotch and water, half-and-half. He stoked the old stove, and fed it with two logs. He sat down for a minute at the kitchen table, feeling too tired to make the effort to go to bed.

Something disturbed the dogs again. Dan swore; if his mother had gone back to sleep they would have woken her once more. He went out to see what was bothering them, leaving the door open. He saw nothing.

When he went back indoors, into the warm smoky kitchen, he had a surprise that caused him to bite his tongue. A small boy stood warming his hands at the range, a very scruffy little boy. He wore dirty plimsolls, dirty jeans, a very dirty sweater. He had dropped a dirty duffle-coat on the floor. His face was dirty.

33

His ears stuck out. His hair had been roughly cut, as though by a drunken amateur. It was shorter than the hair of most little boys of the period.

The little boy said, 'Hullo.'

It was Anna.

Anna said, 'There you are! You didn't recognize me till I spoke.'

It was true. Without the long mop of hair she was transformed into a sharp-faced urchin. Her sticking-out ears, previously hidden, were what you noticed and would remember and would describe.

'You said you were going to tell about that man to the police,' said Dan numbly.

'No I didn't.'

Dan thought for a moment. He decided she was right.

He said, 'You *looked* as though you were going to do like we said.'

'I can't help how I looked. You just thought that was how I looked. I'm not going back to school until that dye wears off. I put on these clothes the minute I went upstairs, and I followed you here.'

'How did you get out of the house?'

'I *live* there. Of *course* I can get out of it. When Mummy locks me in I *have* to be able to get out.'

Dan nodded, too tired to nod. At Anna's age he had constantly climbed in and out of the cottage.

Still he said, 'You must go home. You must talk to the police.'

'I won't. I was out of the house before you were. I waited for you. I snipped off my hair while I waited. I put it all in a paper bag, and I've just burned it in your stove. I saw the car come, when I was hiding. I heard them talking about your bicycle.'

'How do you know it was mine?'

'They said so. One of them said, "I know 'at bike. 'At's Dan bloody Mallett's ruddy bike".' She was being the policeman as accurately as she had been George Barrow.

'You mustn't use words like that,' said Dan.

'I only did because he did, to tell you exactly what he said.

34

"'At's Dan bloody Mallett's ruddy bike". Those were his exact words.'

'You only said it again to give yourself a chance of using a bad word again.'

She giggled. Still being the policeman, she said, "At splosh o' paint on the mudguard. Got reason to remember 'at, I 'ave.'

'Wonder what reason?' murmured Dan. 'Wonder what policeman?'

'They'll think you left it behind because you kidnapped me,' said Anna in her normal, clear, childishly-arrogant, upper-class voice.

It seemed highly probable.

'We'll soon put that right,' said Dan.

'It is right. You have kidnapped me. Well, I've kidnapped you really.'

'I'll escape.'

'I wouldn't, if I were you. I'll say you made an indecent assault at me.' Dan goggled at her. He felt himself goggling. He said, 'Do you know what an indecent assault is, Anna?'

'Call me Cedric.'

'Cedric,' said Dan, everything suddenly too much for him. 'Why Cedric?'

'He's my hero. Lieutenant Cedric Maltravers, Royal Navy. It's a red book, with pictures.'

'Do you know what indecent assault is, Cedric?'

Cedric shrugged. 'Like a foul, I suppose. Like whacking someone on the ankle with your stick when you're playing hockey, or biting someone when you're playing netball. But I'll think of something better for you to have done to me. I think we ought to go now, don't you? If the police know that's your bicycle, I should think they'll be here quite soon.'

'Yes,' said Dan. 'Let's go.'

3

Dan went upstairs to reassure his mother. She was not re-assured. Going out in the middle of the night was unfortunately normal for him, but going out and coming in and going out again meant extra devilments.

'What were all 'at jabberen?' she asked.

'Nipper latched on to me, like. Runnen away from a lar-rupen. Got to return him t'sorrowen kin. 'At's why I'm off.'

'For days, ye say?'

'Likely a few.'

'Get a bit o' peace, I will. Or I would, but for the zoo. So be, we'll manage. Take care.'

'Take care, old lady.'

On the way downstairs, Dan suddenly came to his senses. He had gone through a fog of fatigue and come out the other side into clarity. It was ridiculous that he should be blackmailed by a spoiled brat of nine, whose stories no one would believe.

Julie would by now have repeated to the police Anna's description of the murderer. It was not a great description, but it added up to somebody profoundly unlike Dan. The whole machinery of the law would be looking for a big fat man with a boil on his neck who had somehow come by the knowledge of Sylvia's and Sophie's movements.

Anna's bluff must be called and Anna taken home in the morning. Any other course of action was preposterous, danger-ous, irresponsible, suicidal, and cruel to Sylvia.

Dan thought he must have been exhausted indeed to have thought otherwise, even for a moment.

'There's another thing,' said Anna.

'No, there isn't,' said Dan.

'Yes, there is,' she said.

It seemed the sort of argument that could go on, without development, for ever. But Anna said, 'I won't go back. I will not. I can see from your face what you're thinking. But there is another thing. I didn't tell you before because I wasn't sure, but I've been thinking about it and thinking about it and now I am sure. It's about that man.'

'Boil and all?'

'Yes, of course. I know him by sight. I had a sort of feeling I'd seen him before, but I couldn't think where. But I thought and thought, and now I remember.'

'Where did you see him?' said Dan, as casually as he could.

'I'll tell you if you promise to take me.'

'Wait now. Hold hard. Do you know his name?'

'I might do. I sort of do.'

'Do you know where he lives?'

'Sort of. Roughly.'

'What does that mean?'

'I'll tell you if you promise to take me.'

'The police are who you'll have to tell.'

'Oh no. If I tell *them* anything it'll be *quite* different. It'll be about you and Julie, and you shooting that man.'

Dan felt himself being sucked back into the fog of fatigue from which he thought he had emerged. He felt himself under the thumb of a character stronger than his own.

'I'll take you to find that man,' said Anna. 'Now that I've remembered where I saw him.'

She seemed very sure she could.

Finding that man, having that man pointed out to him by Anna, was certainly the very best thing that could happen. It was the *only* good thing that could happen.

'All right,' said Dan.

'Promise you won't make me go to the police, or home, or to school?'

'You'll have to go in the end.'

'Not till I've got this purple off my arm. Promise? Cross your heart and hope to die?'

'Oh yes,' said Dan. 'Oh yes.'

'Do it, then.'

'Cross my heart and hope to die,' said Dan.

'Come on, or the police will catch you.'

'Might be a nice change,' said Dan. 'All right.'

Dan packed some clothes, a toothbrush and a razor into a rucksack. He folded the clothes carefully.

Anna watched him impatiently. 'You won't need things like that,' she said. 'We're outlaws.'

'Maybe just why we'll need them,' said Dan. 'I wish I had a smart black hat.'

'You'd look silly in a smart black hat,' said Anna.

Dan refilled his flask. He put on a short, heavy workman's coat. He filled the pockets with biscuits. There was nothing else in the larder that suited fugitives. They went out. Dan locked the door, then posted the key in through the letter-box. The act symbolized departure, exile, homelessness.

It was cold. Yet again he quieted the dogs. Anna wanted to get into the kennels with the dogs, saying that they were cold and she would make them warm. Dan won a brief, bitter argument on this proposition only by saying that Pansy, the old pointer, would bite Anna. He realized that without this clincher he would have been overruled. He faced the future with dismay.

He went deep into the Priory Woods behind the cottage. A few paces took him into tangled undergrowth and tree-roots, and to an abandoned rabbit warren. He lifted the camouflage from a rabbit-hole, withdrew a waterproof plastic bag, and took a handful of notes and silver from his Current Account. His Deposit Account, in another rabbit-hole which even he had difficulty finding, was not to be touched for day-to-day needs. He had to use his pencil flash in order to fill his pockets with the unaccustomed jingle of money. Anna consequently saw all that he was doing.

'Is that stolen money?' she asked.

'Good gracious no,' lied Dan. 'All earnings o' the sweat o' my brow.'

It did not matter that he lied, because she did not believe him.

'Now we must go to Stepleton Underhill,' said Anna.

'That's a tidy step.'

'It's where I saw that man.'

'Hum. We'll go there, then. Do you fancy walking nine miles?'

'Of course not. We'll steal a car.'

'Oh yes. Silly of me not to think o' that.'

'Mummy says you stole Grandpapa's car.'

'Borrowed,' said Dan, shocked.

'So you know how to do it.'

They were at the edge of the wood now, on the track between the cottage and the road. There was a glow among the bare branches above them, followed at once, as the source of the sound cleared a barrier, by the noise of an engine.

'Fuzz,' said Anna.

Dan nodded, thinking as he did so that it was a silly thing to do in the dark.

They scrambled back into the cover of the wood. The police car went past them two yards away, and stopped in front of the cottage. The dogs barked.

'They've come because they recognized your bicycle,' whispered Anna. 'It was silly of you to leave it where anybody could see it. It's a good thing you've got me with you now. I wonder what Julie told them?'

Dan wondered too. He wondered who had called the police long before Julie could get around to doing so. He wondered if the police had believed Julie's report of Anna's description of the murderer. He wondered if his bicycle had yet been fingerprinted. He wondered if the man with the boil lived in Stepleton Underhill.

There was a loud knocking on the cottage door. Dan knew his mother would already be awake, because of the dogs. He knew that, if she did decide to go downstairs, she would be a very long time about it. She could not hurry; she would not if she could. She would not face anybody with her hair in a mess. She would brush it and comb it and tie the ends into the little tight bun she wore at the back, stuck with pins like a pomander. Probably she would dress, a weary and protracted performance. Getting downstairs took her a long time, too. The police could cool their heels in the meanwhile. And cool their heels would get, in the chilly small hours.

Dan and Anna crept on to the road and started towards the village. Anna complained almost at once of hunger. Dan fed her biscuits, sparingly, as they walked.

Of course she was quite right about the car. Other crises, on other nights, had caused Dan to make arrangements in the matter of cars. There were consequently several available to him, though they were locked and in locked garages. The most convenient was Mr Potter's at the Old Mill. Dan disliked the Potters. They threw their weight and their money about in the village shop, expecting the village people to stand back out of the way. They had a new Rover, a fast, comfortable car but not an odd or distinctive one. They locked the garage, probably because of the power tools they also kept there. Dan had borrowed the key, had another cut, and returned the original. He had taken the numbers of the car-keys, door and ignition, and bought their twins at a big garage outside Milchester. His three keys were behind a loose brick in the garage wall. It was better to have them there than to carry them about. He had keys to other cars and garages, and they were all kept conveniently on the spot: the point about the Potters' was that it was nearest. Dan was fed up with walking, and Anna had eaten most of the biscuits.

Dan told Anna to wait for him at the mouth of the Potters' drive. She refused to do so, saying she'd be scared left alone in the dark. Although she was a girl, and only nine, Dan flatly disbelieved this. But he could not call her bluff without an altercation that might wake the Potters. She followed him up the grass verge of the drive, avoiding as carefully as he the crunch of the gravel.

The keys were there. The double doors of the garage opened quietly. Dan shut them behind them.

'You mustn't start the car with the doors shut,' said Anna. 'You get something moxide. Gas. It kills you.'

'Only for a moment while we start,' said Dan. 'Once she's running she's lovely and quiet.'

'Oh, have you stolen this one before?'

'Borrowed,' Dan corrected her again.

The car started quickly but far from silently. As soon as it was ticking over, Dan reopened the garage doors. He backed very slowly down the drive. He drove without lights, but not without the Rover's powerful reversing lights. They shone away from the house, but they glared on the gravel and the gateposts. The engine made very little noise, but the tyres crunched on the gravel. Anna was outspokenly critical of Dan's reversing, which she said was too slow and too noisy.

Dan swung the wheel as he cleared the gateposts, backed another ten yards along the road, and stopped. He left the engine running, which was quieter than another start would be.

'Wait here,' he said to Anna. 'I'll just nip up an' shut those doors.'

Anna was out of the car before he was. She followed him up to the garage. They both stood as still as stones, looking and listening for any sign that the removal of the car had been heard.

No lights came on. The sleep of the Old Mill was undisturbed.

Dan shut and locked the garage door. He put the key back in its hiding-place and replaced the brick.

Mr Potter would think it was magic. The police might think it was Mallett.

Dan drove to Stepleton Underhill, which was outside his normal beat and which he knew very little. It was a beauty-spot, a place in summer of tourists and teas. There was a pub where you drank on a lawn which sloped to a river: 'Coaches by Appointment Only'. There was something famous about the church, and there was a National Trust house. The village itself was picturesque to a degree which showed that no villagers lived in it; they had been removed to a council estate out of sight, as the cost of the cottages climbed into the managerial bracket. Some of the old cottages were now antique shops, others the weekend retreats of stockbrokers. It was a funny place to be going.

The man with the boil must come from the council estate. A

burglar with a sawn-off shotgun did not belong in the scrubbed grey stone of the village street.

Anna went to sleep, and Dan very badly wanted to join her. The car's heater was soporific. There was nothing on the radio.

A little short of the village, Dan pulled off the road and bumped up a track, where he thought he remembered a wood. He heaved the car out of the track on to a sort of ride into the trees. The car bumped over roots, and bare twigs scratched at the windows. Anna woke up.

In a voice thick with sleep she said, 'Mummy? Julie?'

Then she was fully awake, and displeased with the bumping and scraping.

Dan stopped and switched off the lights. There was no way of knowing how well the car was hidden until daylight, which might show that it was not hidden at all.

Dan put Anna in the back seat. There was a rug there which he tucked round her. He settled himself in the front passenger seat. He could have slept sitting on a wire fence.

He woke in strengthening daylight. The dashboard clock said it was seven-thirty. He felt thoroughly refreshed, but stiff and with a brown taste in his mouth. He was hungry, and he wanted to brush his teeth and shave. Whether any of these needs could be met was doubtful. He found that his movements were restricted. He was in a straitjacket. He had a moment of unreasoning, sleepy panic.

Fully awake, he found that he was cocooned in the rug he had put round Anna. He struggled out of it and twisted his head. The back of the car was empty.

Anna had gone for a walk. To spend a penny. To spy out the land. To steal food. To look for the man with the boil on his neck. Or simply to give Dan a fright. She had tucked the rug round him, as he had round her, without waking him up. She must have been very gentle, taken time and trouble. He began to see new dimensions in Anna. He found himself worrying about her.

He took stock of the car's position. It was in a wood, but not much of a wood. It was pretty visible from the road, which was nearer than Dan had expected. He had come so slowly up the track that a short distance had seemed a long one. In front of the car, half-right, was a building fifty yards away, sketchily visible through towering brambles.

Dan got out of the car. He yawned, stretched, scratched his head, rubbed his bristly chin, knuckled the remaining sleep out of his eyes. He went forward delicately to see what lay beyond the brambles.

It was the council estate. Two hundred raw red cottages, detached, semi-detached, or in terraces, coming to life as he watched, doors banging, cars starting, chimneys smoking. Dan had parked on the very lip of this teeming area.

He wondered why no children were going off to school or men to work, and then remembered it was Sunday. That cut both ways. Folk not out as early, but more of them about with time on their hands to poke and pry and ask questions.

It might be hours before the Potters at the Old Mill discovered their car was gone; or they might be making an early start to somewhere – Holy Communion, perhaps – or they might not be going anywhere, all day, in which case they might not discover for twenty-four hours or more that the stable was empty, for all its locked door. They might want something else out of the garage, a rake for fallen leaves, or a fork for a bonfire. There were endless possibilities either way. The only safe thing was to assume that the borrowing had already been discovered and the police already informed.

Therefore it was necessary to move the car at once, right away from the council estate into trees that really hid it, into a barn or behind a cowshed, anywhere away from here. That, or abandon the car, sever all connection with it. But assuming the police would assume Dan had taken the car, the car placed him at Stepleton Underhill. He couldn't abandon Stepleton Underhill, because it was where Anna had seen the man with the boil on his neck. Seeing the car, the police would know Dan was near, and with Anna. They must assume he had taken Anna. They must know by now that no one had borrowed his bicycle and left it outside the Old Hall.

Dan played chess in his mind, he white and the police black. Suppose he did leave the car where it could be seen? That eventually brought the police here. The police ought to be looking for a man with a boil on his neck, and this was where that man was, or anyway had been. If it was a good starting-point for Dan, it was a much better one for the police. There were more of them, and they could ask questions openly. 'Yes, George Smith is a big fat man and he's got a bloody great boil on his neck.' 'Thank you, sir.' 'It's my pleasure to do my duty, constable. You'll find George Smith at number 73, probably fast asleep in bed on account of he was up all night shooting holes in Piet Vandervelde.' Anna jumps up out of a ditch and identifies George Smith. Dan remains in the ditch until they all go away.

It was an attractive scenario; Dan examined it for weaknesses. He found about thirty, all fatal. Some centred on the psychology of the police, and some on the psychology of Anna.

The first decision was right: he had to move the car, and quick. But he couldn't, until Anna came back. He could drive the car away, hide it, and return: by which time Anna would probably have come and gone. Suspecting him of treachery, of ditching her, Anna might then, out of pique, go to the police and tell them Dan had murdered the housebreaker whose identity she still didn't know.

He could leave her a note? Somebody else might find it. He had nothing to write with, or on.

Thinking made him hungrier. Only crumbs remained of the biscuits in his coat pocket, mixed with ancient fluff.

'Boo,' said a voice behind him.

For the second time Anna gave Dan such a start that he bit his tongue.

'It was kind of you to wrap me in that blanket,' said Dan.

'Yes, I know. But I didn't need it any more. I went for a walk.'

'I wish you'd told me you were going.'

'You might have tried to stop me. There's a telephone box in the middle of the village. I wanted to ring up Mummy, but I didn't know the number. So I rang up the police station in Medwell.'

'*You what?*'

'There's a telephone book in the box, on a piece of string. Mrs Gundry answered. So I said, "So be as Miss Julie ben 'ome?"'

Anna's voice was, more or less, that of old Dorothy Barrow in the cottage at the Old Hall.

'So,' said Anna, 'Mrs Gundry said, "Who's phonin' Julie at cockcrow?" So I said, "A-ben worken t'college, sweepen an' such. Ben a message f'Miss Julie, right urgent." So Julie came to the telephone, and I said I was safe and well and a lady had kidnapped me, and would she please tell Mummy? I said we were miles away and nobody could find us, and nobody was to try because I was safe and well. Then I said good-bye and hung up. If you talk and talk and talk, they can find out where you are.'

'You said a lady had kidnapped you?'

'Yes. So they'll be looking for a lady with a little girl, not a man with a little boy.'

'That,' said Dan reluctantly, 'was clever.'

'Yes I know. So then I went to the Bed and Breakfast.'

Dan blinked at her. He began to be sure that he had not had nearly enough sleep.

'It's on the edge of the village, at the far end,' said Anna. 'It's called Clematis Farm, Bed and Breakfast. I don't think it's really a farm at all. It's a lovely place. Fancy having breakfast in bed.'

'You went there?'

'Yes, of course. I told them my name –'

'*You what?*'

'Cedric Maltravers. I said my father was coming along in a minute with the car. I said you were stopping at the pub on the way.'

'Pub's shut. Why would I stop there?'

'To go to the loo.'

'Ah.'

'I said we wanted a room for a few days. Bed and breakfast. We have to have the other meals out. But they're cooking breakfast for us now. Eggs and bacon and sausages and chips. Do you like tea or coffee? I said coffee, but I don't suppose it

45

will be very good. There's a bath if you want one. It's high time you shaved, too.'

'I know,' said Dan humbly.

'You can put the car in a garage behind, so the police can't see it.'

'Thank you,' said Dan. 'Am I Mr Maltravers?'

'Captain Maltravers. Would you rather be army or navy?'

'Royal Marines,' said Dan wildly. 'Let's go, then.'

'Not until you've changed.'

'Changed.'

'Yes, of course.'

And of course she was right. Only a Marines captain of dangerous eccentricity would dress as Dan was dressed. The knapsack held clothes from a different world.

Awkwardly, in the back of the car, Dan changed into a neat poplin shirt, dark tie, blue suit, black shoes. Anna kept her face firmly averted. The suit was wrinkled from the knapsack, but that could be explained by a long drive at night. His unruly, mousy hair was out of character, but beyond attempting to flatten it with his hands there was nothing he could do about that, without bottles of substances he did not have. As a matter of fact his whole get-up was out of character – he looked like a tousled, unshaven, assistant bank manager, not a Captain of Marines – but the Stepleton Underhill Bed and Breakfast might not be alert to such subtleties.

'What a slowcoach you are,' said Anna. 'I can change in fifty-seven seconds. You were right though – you ought to have a smart black hat.'

Captain Maltravers made a moderate impression at Clematis Farm Bed and Breakfast. Mr Potter's Rover made a good one. The knapsack, as their only luggage, would have made a bad one, but Bed and Breakfast was more used to people with knapsacks than to Captains of Royal Marines, and saw no incongruity.

'Had a suitcase stolen out of the car yesterday,' said Dan in his banker's voice, which he tried to make as much as possible like a Captain's voice. 'We'll kit Cedric out a bit better when the shops open tomorrow.'

'I don't need much kit, Pater,' said Cedric.

'Pater' was more than Dan was prepared to take. He gave Cedric an awful look. Cedric looked back guilelessly.

The car was stowed in a garage out of sight of the road.

Dan brushed his teeth and shaved, and had a quick but blissful bath. Trusting that an adequate first impression had been made, he resumed his normal clothes, but with the tie. He realized he ought to be smoking a pipe.

He and Cedric had a heavy, greasy, and delicious breakfast. Cedric's forebodings about the coffee were justified. Mrs Chambers the proprietress produced the breakfast, explaining that the girl was off because it was out of season.

'I don't normally do this,' she said. 'Wait on customers meself. You mustn't think I normally do this, Captain er.'

She was painfully refined. Dan, also painfully refined, thought the two of them were like actors in a play. Their audience was too busy with breakfast to appreciate the performance.

Labouring to sustain his character, Dan asked for a *Sunday Telegraph*. To his relief, none was available.

'Last week,' he said, 'there was a most interesting article, by the medical correspondent, about boils.'

'Nasty things,' said Mrs Chambers. 'Mr Chambers was a martyr.'

'Often a matter of diet, apparently,' said Dan. 'Something in the ground, just locally you know, something in the vegetables.'

'Daresay,' said Mrs Chambers. 'It's wonderful what they do find out.'

'If your husband was a martyr, there'd be other people hereabouts suffering, too?'

'Daresay,' said Mrs Chambers. 'They cover them up, mostly.'

She knew of no one in the village currently suffering from a boil on the back of the neck.

After breakfast Dan borrowed scissors and addressed himself to Cedric's hair.

'It's worse, not better,' said Cedric.

'More like a boy,' suggested Dan.

'More like a scarecrow,' said Cedric, doing herself an injustice. 'What shall we do now?'

'Look for a man with a boil on his neck,' said Dan.

They strolled through the council estate, quartering it, until they were in danger of attracting attention for choosing so peculiar a place for a walk. They saw no one with a boil. They saw many large fat men; Cedric saw none she recognized.

They returned to Bed and Breakfast, Dan having had an idea. He borrowed from Mrs Chambers a square of lint and a few inches of sticking-plaster. He said that he had hurt his leg in a steeplechase. The steeplechase was heavily overplaying his role, but it slipped out and he had to stick with it.

In their bedroom, Dan loosened his tie and taped the lint to the back of his neck.

'Conversational openings,' he explained.

At twelve-thirty they went to the Anchor, where the lawn sloped to the river. It was not the weather for the lawn, but there was a dining-room. Dan deposited Cedric at a table in the dining-room and went into the public bar. It was not the right bar for his character, but it was right for news of his quarry.

He ordered a pint of bitter, complaining about his neck. He turned down his coat collar, so that the dressing was visible; he moved his head stiffly, as though his neck was sore.

The barmaid did not react with immediate gossip about a regular who was suffering from the same affliction; nor did the landlord; nor did any of the dozen people in the bar.

There was one particularly big young man in the bar, without a boil on his neck. He was known to the others, but not quite of their fellowship. Something set him apart. He was in ordinary clothes – a heavy cardigan, flannel trousers – but there was something smart about him. His hair was close-cropped and well brushed. He had a small moustache. Dan thought he was a soldier. Perhaps a Marine. Dan kept quiet about the Marines. The big young man was staring at Dan; He was pretending not to do so, but he was definitely staring. It was not recognition. Dan was sure he had never seen the man before.

The big young man got up. He murmured to the landlord, who nodded. Dan heard the word 'phone'. The man went through a door into the back premises.

'Frank's on the prowl,' said somebody.

'Law never sleeps,' said somebody.

Law. Prowl. Small moustache, air of belonging in uniform. Staring. Dan did the sum with great speed and a sick feeling. The big man was the local policeman. He had been told, first thing in the morning, by telephone, to keep an eye out for a murderer with a boil on his neck. Dan was a stranger with a boil on his neck. Dan was on the point of being arrested for murder.

4

Dan made a bolt – an inconspicuous, apologetic bolt like that of a shy man suddenly requiring the Gents. He passed the door of the Gents, for he had no need of the facility, and no wish to be caught in a cul-de-sac. It was the first place a zealous policeman would try for a fugitive murderer in a pub.

In the passage between the public bar and the dining-room, Dan pulled off the dressing on the back of his neck. The plaster was firmly stuck to the short hairs on his nape, and he almost screamed as he ripped it off. Had he had a boil in truth, the pain would have been excruciating.

He passed another door, beside which stood a pair of green rubber gumboots, which somebody obviously used for gardening. They gave him an idea so excellent that he decided to risk the loss of time and the threat of cul-de-sac. He ran back to the Gents with the boots. As in many pretentious pubs, the Gents let down the decor and the atmosphere. One wall was lined with what ought to have been porcelain but which resembled the surface of a road; there were two cubicles, the doors starting a foot above the floor and ending six feet above it; and over all hung a smell at once human and chemical. The room was empty, or Dan would have dropped the boots and run away immediately. But he went into the further cubicle. He put the boots side by side in front of the pan so that, to anybody peeping below the door, a man would appear to be sitting there. He locked the door, and then climbed out over it. There was a window with a single hinged catch: he went out through it into the chilly, deserted garden, and damaged another lavender hedge. He took a stiff new five-pound note out of his hip pocket, and with the note, twice folded lengthwise, he held back the catch while he closed the window from outside. When he withdrew the note the catch fell into its slot. He had not used a banknote for this purpose before, but it answered.

The whole ruse was primitive stuff, but Dan thought it would give them time.

He trotted to the dining-room, and entered it from the garden door. The dining-room was generally blond, shiny, and hung with sporting prints. Cedric was perched at the table where Dan had left her, studying a large menu. During Dan's absence a cold buffet had been spread on a table by the wall. It was not the weather for a cold buffet, but the food looked good. Cedric evidently thought so: she was chewing a too-large mouthful, while pretending not to. Whatever servant had produced the buffet had disappeared for more.

'We have to go,' said Dan.

'Why? Look at all that food. I'm hungry.'

'A lot of policemen are about to chase us.'

'Then it won't matter a few more people chasing us,' said Cedric.

She picked up a paper table-napkin, ran to the buffet, and loaded the napkin with slices of pork, bread, most of a Brie, and some kind of sticky pudding. She handed the bundle to Dan just as the waiter re-entered the dining-room. Dan got the bundle into his cap before the waiter saw it. He did not like being the receiver of these particular stolen goods, but it was no time to argue the point.

'Just going to take a stroll in the garden,' he said with false heartiness to the waiter. 'Work up an appetite, what?'

Adding 'what?' to a remark of this kind, or any kind, was something he had never done before; it made him feel like a man with patent-leather hair, a monocle, and plus-fours in a fierce check.

The waiter, a youth from Southern Europe, was apathetic about Dan's plans for a walk in the garden. Indeed he might not have understood. He watched without expression as Dan followed Cedric out into the garden, and turned back to the buffet. He gave a shout. He had just arranged everything, and it was not as he had left it. He noticed, no doubt, that there was less pork, less bread, less pudding, and almost no Brie.

'Quick,' said Cedric.

She ran round the side of the pub to the front. She there stopped so suddenly that Dan cannoned into her. Dan saw why. A police car had just drawn up in front of the pub. Two plain-clothes men were getting out of it. A uniformed driver stayed where he was. The plain-clothes men hurried into the pub. Dan imagined them banging on the door of the cubicle in the Gents.

There was commotion behind them: a shout of rage in a Latin language. The police driver sat in his car commanding the whole of the front of the pub.

To Dan's horrified amazement, Cedric ran straight to the police car and to the driver's open window.

'Oh sir, please sir,' she said, terror in her little high voice, 'there's a dangerous lunatic coming after us with a knife.'

'Quite true, officer,' said Dan, in the voice (nearly) of Captain Maltravers RM. 'Some sort of Dago. Mad as Dick's hatband.'

The police driver looked startled at the phrase which, indeed, startled Dan himself. He began to climb out of his car. The waiter rounded the corner at this moment. He shouted when he saw Dan and Cedric.

'Oh, save us, please sir!' whimpered Cedric.

The policeman advanced to meet the waiter, who tried to run round him, still shouting. The policeman caught the waiter by the arm. The waiter struggled. He pointed furiously at Dan and Cedric. His English had broken down.

'Now we'll go and have lunch,' said Cedric.

'This is all too much for me,' said Dan.

'That's all right. I'll eat most of it, if you like.'

She did, too.

It amazed people that Dan had such a prodigious appetite, while remaining so lithe and slight. It amazed Dan himself. He could not imagine where, in his wiry and narrow-boned frame, the great quantities of beef, pheasant, potatoes and vegetables managed to find room. But his gastronomic exploits were nothing to Cedric's. He watched her in astonishment. She ate with her fingers, rapidly, alternating pork, bread, Brie and sticky pudding. A purist might have said that she put too much in her mouth at once. Dan would certainly have said that the sticky pudding, which combined caramel, cream and some kind of jam, would have been better kept distant from the meat and cheese. But Cedric liked her alternate mouthfuls.

Some of the sticky pudding had leaked through the paper table-napkin on to the lining of Dan's cap. He did not realize this until he put his cap on and then tried to remove it.

They ate in chilly sunshine in a clearing in a wood. They had seen and heard no more of the police.

'I made a mistake this morning,' said Dan.

Cedric nodded, with her mouth full.

'That wodge of lint, like I had a boil – it seemed like a good idea, but it was a sight too clever. I somehow never thought to bring down a swarm of bluebottles on myself. I should have foreseen that. I can't think why I didn't. My brains are scrambled. It's too much excitement.'

Cedric finished her mouthful. She appeared to consider, for a moment, the alternatives of replying to Dan or filling her mouth again. Breaking with precedent, she ate a piece of pork with on it a lump of Brie and on that a dollop of sticky pudding.

It was the last of the Brie. Dan had been hoping for a bit. He had become fond of the cheeses of Normandy when he ate dainty candle-lit dinners with genteel girls in his years at the bank in Milchester. Brie never came his way now. He conceded that Cedric's need, as a growing girl, was greater than his own; it remained startling that Cedric needed more food, and could accommodate it.

'This being where you saw your bloke,' said Dan, 'it's where we ought to stick around. But I can't exactly flaunt myself after what happened at the pub. I can't imagine that they'll come prying at the Bed and Breakfast, so we're safe there another night or two, I think. It's not where a killer on the run would hide. Nor's the public bar at the Anchor, come to that . . . The Potters must've spotted their car's gone by now, so we can't use it in daylight. Supposing your chap's gone away? Suppose he's in Scotland? Suppose he was just visiting here?'

Cedric's mouth was too full to answer, but after she had swallowed she said, 'He works here.'

'Where?'

'In one of the shops. An antique shop. Mummy stopped on the way through, to look at some awful old chairs.'

'Why didn't you tell me this before?'

But Cedric had refilled her mouth, and it was a little time before she said, 'I've only just remembered.'

'You didn't talk to the man?'

'No. I didn't get out of the car. Mummy talked to him. She didn't buy the chairs. She said they were too expensive.'

'Can you remember which shop?'

'I can't remember what it was called. I expect I'll remember when I see it. I'll go and look, shall I? When I've finished my lunch.'

Dan nodded. It was all turning out easier than he had dared hope. If Cedric confidently identified a man in an antique shop as the one she had seen in the hall of her home, they were home and dry. The antique shop rang sufficiently true: the Old Hall was full of valuable things, things saleable to tourists passing through Stepleton Underhill. Dan himself knew an antique dealer in Milchester who bought things from him, rather cheaply, without asking questions. From that to pinching the things was no great jump. For all Dan knew, all antique dealers did it. It was a good Socialistic arrangement, the redistribution of antiques. Presumably the police would find out, with all their facilities for snooping, how this antique dealer knew that Sylvia and her terrifying dog were going to be away that night.

An antique dealer could get a boil on his neck as well as anybody else, Dan supposed. Not enough exercise, probably. An antique dealer with a sawn-off shotgun was a bit odder.

'I'm sure he had a beard,' said Cedric suddenly.

'You weren't sure before. You said his head was turned away.'

'Not directly away. No, I wasn't sure before, but I am now.'

A fat antique dealer with a beard: that sounded likely. If you had to imagine an antique dealer, Dan thought, you'd picture someone fat, with a beard. Very likely with a scarf drawn through a ring, instead of a tie. Very likely with sandals. The picture sharpened. The sawn-off shotgun fitted with it less and less, but that was one thing there was no doubt about.

'Are you going to remember more things you weren't sure about before?' asked Dan.

'I expect so,' said Cedric. 'I'll think and think and think.'

She did so, for a short time, until she became visibly bored with thinking. Then she said she would go into the village and look at the antique shops. They would be closed, as it was Sunday and out of season, but she would remember which one was the right one.

'Don't go near the Anchor,' said Dan. 'The crazy man might see you.'

'I could disguise myself as a little girl,' said Cedric, 'if I had a skirt.'

Dan thought not. Cedric looked too completely like a little boy ever to be mistaken for a girl.

'Be careful,' said Dan. 'I'll wait for you here.'

'Yes, of course,' said Cedric.

The early afternoon sun warmed the air and the ground. Dan lay back and looked at the sky. He wanted to make plans, but it was impossible to look further ahead than the next step or two. Cedric would identify the shop, no doubt, but she would probably not see the man. They would peep at the man in the morning, Dan as well as Cedric keeping well away from the Anchor. Then they would telephone. Bed and Breakfast would be a safe haven for tonight. Supper had better be bought some distance away: they could risk the car in the dark. It was all straightforward.

Two pairs of bullfinches were busy in the trees around the clearing, going *whib-whib* and looking for the buds of the spring growth, the new leaves and flowers which would not unfurl for five months but which were already little succulent knobs for the birds to peck at. Far above, seagulls were flying inland, looking for food in fresh plough or landlocked water. Ragged parties of starlings were flying into the wind, dead straight, fast and purposeful. Dan felt equally purposeful and equally sure of his direction and destination.

He closed his eyes. The sunlight was red through his lids. He wondered whether he could risk going to sleep, and, while doing so, went to sleep.

He was woken by cold and by the sensation of eyes on him. When he opened his own eyes he found that the other eyes were Cedric's. The sun was low. The clearing was in deep shadow, but the topmost twigs of the surrounding trees were gilded by the sunset. Dan thought it was a little after six. He supposed Cedric was hungry again.

'I could have killed you,' said Cedric. 'You must always post a sentry.'

Dan examined the logic of this, for a moment. He let it go, and nodded submissively.

Cedric said she had found the right antique shop. It had a red sign. It had a silly name, which she had forgotten, but there was no mistaking it because of the sign.

She said, 'I rang up Mummy.'

'Oh yes?'

'Sophie was married. I wonder how many puppies she'll have.'

'How's your mother?'

'In a frightful tizz about the man being murdered and me being kidnapped.'

'Did she tell you who the man was?'

'No. Poor man. But I s'pose it must have been quick. Mummy asked me where I was, but I said I didn't know. I said we drove a long way in the dark. That was quite true, wasn't it? I said I was getting enough to eat, which was a bit of a fib, and the lady who kidnapped me made me brush my teeth.'

'That was a fib, too.'

'Mummy said, do you want money?'

'Do *I* want money?'

'No, silly. Does the lady who kidnapped me want money. *Do* you want some money? I expect Mummy will give you some, in return for me. What do you think I'm worth? A million million pounds?'

'Thereabouts,' said Dan.

'Yes, that's what I thought. I told Mummy it wasn't Julie's fault I was kidnapped.'

'That was a good idea.'

'Yes, I know. I said Julie was busy not disturbing the scene of the crime, so the lady climbed in and kidnapped me. Then I said somebody was coming, so I hung up. That was so they couldn't find out where I was talking from.'

'Were you in the phone box in the middle of the village?'

'Telephone box.'

'Sorry.'

'Yes, of course, where else could I telephone from? But don't worry, nobody paid any attention to me. I was very careful, all the time. I didn't go to sleep where anybody could have found me and killed me or arrested me. Where shall we have dinner? Can we go to the Sleepy Cow in Belminster? I've asked and asked Mummy to take me there but she says it's too expensive. If we go there you'd better put your suit on again. It's a pity you haven't got a uniform.'

'It's near enough a uniform,' said Dan, thinking of men in banks.

Belminster was another famous village. People usually thought 'minster' meant cathedral, and stared with disappointment at the red Victorian church which had been rebuilt by a misguided philanthropist. But 'minster' used to mean monastery, and there had been one, which was abolished with all the rest by Henry VIII and its stones used for mansion, parsonage, and piggery. Some of the stones had enlarged the house at the end of the village which, converted at startling expense in 1960, was now the whimsically named Sleepy Cow, a restaurant which appeared in the good food guides.

Dan thought it was pretty good. Cedric had been right to make him change. Cedric wanted champagne, and was distinctly underdressed for the Sleepy Cow, but the management treated her with indulgence.

'What will young sir have to follow?' said the waiter.

Cedric giggled, with her mouth full. She had strawberry

meringues. Dan felt indulgent, too, as the adventure was coming to an end.

Sylvia was right that it was too expensive.

'"Bed and Breakfast" means both together,' said Cedric in the morning.

'Under the same roof,' said Dan.

'No. It doesn't say "Bed. And. Breakfast". It says "Bedand-breakfast". That means breakfast in bed. Mummy never lets me have breakfast in bed unless I'm so ill I don't want any breakfast. That's why I wanted to *come* here, just to have breakfast in bed.'

'Your breakfast is waiting for you downstairs,' said Dan, trying, for the first time, the dangerous experiment of being firm with Cedric. 'Come down or go without. Myself, I'm going down. I'm hungry.'

Cedric came down very quickly and very crossly.

'Something Lieutenant Cedric Maltravers would never do,' said Dan, 'is have breakfast in bed.'

'Yes, he did. When he was on leave. As a change from getting up at six bells in the dogwatch. He had bachelor chambers. He sat up in bed in a silk dressing-gown, and his man brought him eggs and mutton chops and muffins and coffee. There's a picture of it. His dressing-gown is beautiful.'

'You have to have the dressing-gown,' said Dan. 'It's no good without the dressing-gown.'

'I could borrow a dressing-gown from Mrs Thingummy,' said Cedric. 'You could be my man. What exactly are muffins?'

'Can't get them nowadays,' said Dan. 'Lost art. It's no good without muffins.'

Dan paid the bill, which for one night and two breakfasts was less than the price of a single dish at the Sleepy Cow. The proprietress was almost too refined to make out the bill and sweep away the money, but not quite. Dan arranged to leave his car in the garage until midday.

'In the season,' said the proprietress, 'we generally bring our customers breakfast in their rooms. It seems more trouble but it's easier really. There's many does appreciate breakfast in bed. It makes a nice change for them.'

Dan had dressed as a banker, in order to confuse the waiter at the Anchor if by chance that excitable fellow should see them. He wished he had a disguise at least as good for Cedric, whose bright yellow hair and sticking-out ears made her distinctive. He tried to get Cedric to wear his cap, but Cedric objected to the vestiges of sticky pudding in the lining.

They walked into the middle of the village, Dan looking warily out for the wronged waiter, the tough young policeman who had seen his boil-dressing, and the police driver.

'There's the shop,' said Cedric.

There it was, red sign and all: 'Ships and Sealingwax' – a gracious jumble of wrought-iron garden furniture on the paved yard in front, a glimpse of vases and samplers through the pebble glass of the windows.

Dan pushed open the door. He went into a smell of furniture polish, lavender and French cigarettes. A woman rose from a tapestry chair, putting down a copy of *Herbalist Monthly*. She wore a kind of tweed caftan, had grey hair no longer than Cedric's, and things on chains round her neck.

'Good morning, good morning,' said Dan, a hearty yet cultured Captain of Marines. 'Is the gentleman here, the one I spoke to some time ago about some chairs?'

'There has never been a gentleman here,' said the caftan lady. 'I dree my own weird.'

'Big chap, with a beard,' said Dan.

'Not even such a one. A customer, perhaps.'

'Ah. Possible. A misunderstanding. Have you a large, bearded customer?'

'No doubt. All manner of men beat a path to this door. Were you looking for chairs? This set of four is attractive.'

'This *is* where we saw the gentleman with the beard, isn't it, Cedric?' said Dan.

But Cedric was staring out of the window, between two tall Staffordshire cats. She turned, wide-eyed, and in a loud whisper said, 'He's just gone by.'

'Walking?'

'On a bike.'

'Are you sure?'

'Yes, of course.'

'A moment,' said Dan, hearty yet courteous, to the lady.

He dashed out of the shop with Cedric. There was no bicycle to be seen.

'He went that way,' said Cedric, pointing.

That way was a sharp corner. Going that way, their man must just have gone out of sight. Dan ran to the corner, and looked round the side of what he realized, unhappily, was the police station. A burly figure was bicycling away, leaving the village for open country at moderate speed. His collar was turned up. He might be bearded, and might have a boil on his neck. Anyway, Cedric had positively recognized him.

'We'll have to risk the car,' said Dan.

They ran in the opposite direction, to Bed and Breakfast. Dan's knapsack was already in the car and the car-keys in his pocket. Dan disliked the idea of going through the middle of a populous village, past its police station, in the middle of a brilliant morning, in a large stolen car. The village bobby knew his face and would certainly by now have the number of the car. He probably had a description of Dan as the probable thief of the car. All that had to be risked.

Dan drove with an air of magnificent innocence past the Anchor and the church and the police station. It occurred to him that he was compounding his other crimes by driving without a licence. He had never had such a thing.

They left the village without a whistle blown. The road dipped and rose, the bottom of the valley invisible. The cyclist reappeared from the invisibility of the valley, labouring up the hill beyond. Dan thought it must be painful for his boil. Obviously he had been a customer in the antique shop, and had been mistaken by Sylvia for someone who worked there. Was that possible? He looked, in the distance, like a labourer, like a man who worked on the roads or the drains or on a building-site, not like a customer of 'Ships and Sealingwax'. A man in a workman's coat on a bicycle would not be a purchaser of that overpriced floss. What had fitted so well was coming apart. But no doubt these oddities would be resolved, when they knew and the police knew who the man was.

Dan went after him slowly, keeping him in sight, keeping an eye on his rear mirror.

When he got to the top of the next hill, he saw, looking ahead, the bicyclist climbing still another hill; he saw, behind, a police car leaving the village.

5

After a moment of instinctive horror, Dan saw how every loose end could be tied up at one go. Since they were chasing the murderer, it was highly convenient to have a police car after them. The thing to do was to overtake and stop the bicyclist just as the police car came up. The police would stop. Cedric would identify the bicyclist as the murderer, and they would all go home for lunch, except the murderer, who would go somewhere else.

Dan accelerated. This took him down the forward slope of the hill and out of sight of the police car. The bicyclist was just going out of sight at the top of the next hill. Dan stormed up the hill, just glimpsing in his mirror, as he reached the crest, the police car on the previous crest. A little way in front, on the verge on the left, the bicyclist was dismounting. Dan braked hard. The man looked at them curiously. Dan got a good look at his face. He was not a man, but a boy of fifteen, overgrown, overfed, beardless, spotty. He was not a workman; he had nothing to do with any antique shop; he had never been a customer at an antique shop.

'That's never him,' said Dan.

'No,' said Cedric, looking very disappointed. 'I thought it was, but it's not.'

The boy dumped his bicycle, a very new and shiny one, on the broad grass verge. He went up a track into a new plantation of fir trees.

'We'll borrow the bike,' said Dan.

They scrambled out of the car. Dan struggled into the straps of his rucksack as they ran back to the bicycle. The boy had disappeared. In wishing to be out of their sight, he had put them out of his own sight. Dan felt bad about taking his bicycle, but probably the police would give him a lift. If not, the walk would do him good. Dan picked up the bicycle and lifted it on to the road. Cedric climbed on to the little baggage carrier over the rear wheel. She grabbed Dan round the waist, and Dan sped away down the hill, pedalling furiously and then free-wheeling when he was going too fast to keep up with the pedals.

'Whee,' said Cedric.

The police in the car had probably not seen the bicycle, which had been far ahead of them and mostly out of sight on the hills. If they had seen it, it could only have been fleetingly and from a distance. They would not notice a change of rider. If they saw it now they would ignore it. They were not chasing men on bicycles, but car-thieves.

But the moment they had talked to the boy, they would know what had happened and come after the bicycle.

The road flattened, then began to ascend sharply. Bicycling up it became hard work, especially with the knapsack and with Cedric clinging. They slowed from a rush to a crawl. They were in full view from three-quarters of a mile behind them.

'That's enough of that,' said Dan.

He jumped off and lifted Cedric off. He heaved the smart new bicycle over the hedge at the side of the road, and followed it, helping Cedric over too. They squatted behind the hedge. It had lost most of its leaves, but they were in pretty good cover. They waited for the police car to go by.

'How,' said Dan, 'did you manage to think that lad was the bloke you saw the night before last?'

'I didn't.'

'Eh?'

'Don't say "eh", it's common. The man I saw from the shop *was* the man. The one we were following was the wrong one.'

'Hum,' said Dan. 'The man you saw went round the corner, out of sight, then into a house, maybe, or up an alleyway between houses . . . And we followed that lad, drawing a swarm of bluebottles along with us . . .'

'He's only a schoolboy,' said Cedric. 'He ought to be at school. It's Monday.'

'Look who's talking.'

'But I'm doing something important. I'm catching murderers.'

'Up to a point,' said Dan.

He considered the point they were at. The murderer at this moment was in Stepleton Underhill. It seemed probable, though it was not certain, that he lived there or thereabouts, since Cedric had seen him there twice. He lived in, or had business in, or had a friend in, one of the few houses in the village this side of the police station.

'We know where your bloke is,' said Dan slowly, 'or was until a minute ago, within about fifty yards. You can tell about him, and they can catch him for sure. Bob's your uncle.'

'No,' said Cedric, 'my uncle is called Ralph, only he isn't a proper uncle. He's going to give me a dog.'

'He gave your Mum a dog.'

'Sophie, yes, of course. He's going to give me a little dog, a terrier to go ratting with.'

'Quite right. Every boy ought to have a dog.'

'I'm not a boy, silly.'

'Oh no,' said Dan, confused. 'I was forgetting.'

'Uncle Ralph gave Mummy a special telephone number, a special secret one, so she could reach him if he disappeared.'

'Why would he disappear?'

'People often want to disappear. I've disappeared. You've often disappeared. Uncle Ralph sometimes disappears to get away from his mother and his sister. He doesn't tell them where he goes, and won't give them his secret telephone number.'

'How do you know all this?'

'I was under the sofa when he was telling Mummy. He gave her his secret telephone number on a bit of paper. That shows he likes Mummy almost as much as he likes me.'

'Yes. Well, that's another topic for another day. What we'll do now is stop the police car and tell them about your bloke in Stepleton.'

'If you stop that police car,' said Cedric, 'I'll tell them you shot that man, because he caught you marrying Julie.'

'Why?'

'Because I've still got purple on my arm.'

'Oh, they won't mind about that. You'll be a hero.'

'Yes, I know but *you* don't know what they're like at school. There's Mummy, too. There's my midnight feast I had. I wish I had a feast now, I'm hungry.'

There was no budging Cedric. Appeal, argument, and threat were equally useless. Without Cedric, Dan was helpless – he could point at a thousand big fat bearded men with boils, in utter ignorance of their doings on Saturday night. Only Cedric could point with confidence at the right man. She could also point with apparent confidence at a lot of other men, most notably at Dan. Whose bicycle, covered with his own finger-prints and nobody else's, had been outside the Old Hall when Piet Vandervelde was killed. Who had disappeared, who was on the run. Who was a bad character and the biggest villain unhung . . .

'We won't stop the police car,' said Dan.

'I know,' said Cedric.

The police car went by, fast. They could not see who was in it, but it seemed likely that the bicycle's owner was. After a certain distance, it would become obvious to the men in the car that the bicycle had left the road. The car would then return, much more slowly, the men inside looking not for a bicyclist on the road but for a lurker in the ditch.

Dan and Cedric had to get back to the village, without being seen. Stepleton Underhill might be no place to be, but it was the necessary place to be.

'I've just remembered something,' said Cedric.

Dan was becoming used to this. It remained valuable: Cedric's memory was intermittent, but at its best it produced good stuff. It was like a lucky dip at a fair, or a fruit machine in a pub. Dan waited for a jackpot.

'That man on the bicycle,' said Cedric, 'I know it was the man I saw at home.'

'Yes.'

'I don't know if it helps. But he was carrying something. On a strap, over his shoulder. It was glasses.'

'Glasses?' Dan repeated stupidly, picturing first beakers for wine or beer, then horn-rimmed spectacles, hanging on a string round the bicyclist's neck.

'Field glasses,' said Cedric. 'Bino . . . binococulars.' She looked expectantly at Dan. Dan stared blankly back. The man was a bird-watcher? A peeping Tom?

'I think they're called race-glasses,' said Cedric.

The penny dropped, not before time, ringing a cheerful bell. It was a jackpot indeed. Nuggets of hope poured out of the machine into Dan's outstretched hands.

Igton races!

Igton was a scruffy little course, deeply provincial, putting on jumping only, well below the level of Wincanton or Newton Abbot or Devon and Exeter. It had been allowed by the Levy Board to survive only because its death would have left so large an area with no race-course at all. There was no money for rebuilding the decrepit grandstand; meetings were always on weekdays; the crowds were thin, the prizes small, the horses on a scale from bad to terrible. Igton attracted retired colonels and layabouts. It had often attracted Dan in the past, though he did not quite fall into either of these categories.

There was a two-day meeting in October, Monday and Tuesday of the last week of the month. This Monday. This very day.

'He was getting a lift to the races,' said Dan slowly. 'Came on his bike to his mate's house, dumped the bike, got in the car.'

'We'll easily see him at the races,' said Cedric.

'Maybe. A big meeting on a Saturday we likely wouldn't, but a little meeting on a Monday we likely will. Twelve miles away. First race two o'clock. We need another car.'

Dan considered going back to the village on the borrowed bicycle. He decided against it – the risk was too great and the first hill too steep – so they walked.

'Can we have lunch at the races?' said Cedric.

Dan thought they could.

Their own car (Mr Potter's car) had disappeared: driven back to the village by a spare policeman, no doubt.

By the time they reached the edge of the village, Cedric was complaining of fatigue and hunger. Dan said that if they had stopped the police car, she could have had a lift and a meal. Cedric said not while her arm was still purple, not unless they actually caught the murderer.

Cedric accepted that catching the murderer would get her out of trouble. Dan was not sure if the same applied to himself.

The car-park beside the Anchor was in some ways the worst place to go, but on balance still the best. The waiter in the dining-room would be busy: if scarred by the rape of his buffet the previous day, he would more likely guard his merchandise than spy on the car park. The police would be highly unlikely to expect Dan's reappearance, here of all places. In the car-park of a popular pub at lunch-time, strangers came and went in new Jaguars and old Minis. In the country, some of the cars were left unlocked. All you needed was gall and luck. He and Cedric had plenty of gall between them, and till now it seemed they had struck lucky, too.

They continued lucky. A BMW, unlocked but without keys in the ignition, yielded a plastic badge for the Members' Car-park at Igton race-course. A Volvo provided a brown felt hat, which Dan thought would make him look slightly less like an assistant bank manager and slightly more like a race-goer. A Ford Fiesta was ready to drive away. Dan drove it away. There was a good chance they would be in the race-course car-park before the owner finished his lunch.

'Can we see the horses?' said Cedric. 'Can we have lunch? Can I lead a horse in? Can I give it a lump of sugar? Can I talk to a jockey?'

'We can see all the horses,' said Dan. 'We can have a bite.'

'I've never been to the races. Mummy doesn't like it. She says it's boring. She says everybody's known for years and years that one horse can run faster than another.'

'Ah, but which one?' said Dean. 'That's the interesting part.'

'Shall we have lots of bets?'

'Might try a nibble. I don't know what's running.'

'I expect we'll win a lot of money.'

'Likely.'

'I expect we'll win a million pounds.'

'Thereabouts,' said Dan, in order to keep the peace.

They came out of a side road, where Dan felt safe, on to a main road, where he felt unsafe. There was a moderate stream of traffic bound for the race-course. There was no police road-block.

The plastic badge from the BMW, now on the Ford's windscreen, carried them unchallenged into the Members' Car-park. It was not full.

Adjoining the car-park was a large marquee, with a banner over the entrance reading 'Blackmore'. Blackmore was a local brewer. Blackmore was entertaining a lot of people in his marquee, from which a merry noise could be heard. Dan assumed that the brewery was sponsoring a race and was taking the opportunity to lush up its trade buyers and licensees, as did Schweppes, Hennessey and others on more glorious occasions at more fashionable courses. Two solid men in uniform were guarding the door into the marquee, looking at invitations and ticking off names on a list. Cedric wanted to go into the marquee, but Dan said they couldn't go in because they hadn't been asked to the party. Cedric thought this unreasonable and unfair.

Beyond the marquee were the race-course stables, and beyond them the field where the horse-boxes were parked.

'Let's go away in one of them,' said Cedric.

'Borrow a horse-box? No, I don't think we'll do that. What about the poor horses, left behind?'

'We'll borrow them too.'

'I don't think we'll do that,' said Dan, anticipating trouble later.

In spite of these disappointments, Cedric was enthralled by the races. Dan bought them day badges for the Members' Enclosure. This was partly to match the manner that went with the suit he happened to be wearing, and the furry brown felt hat from Bond Street out of the Volvo. It was partly that he had no real idea what class of man they were looking for – a denizen of the Members' at £6, Tattersalls at £3.50, the Silver Ring for £1, the course for nothing. With badges for the Members', they could go freely down the socio-economic scale, tactfully searching everywhere. More economically badged, they could not go up the scale, their way through various gates being barred by men with metal badges and bowler hats.

Cedric's badge was half-price. She wore it proudly, nevertheless. Dan bought her a racecard, took her to the bar under the grandstand, and bought what he thought must be enough hot sausage rolls for them both. They were enough for Cedric. Dan stood in line again, looking round constantly for a man to fit Cedric's description. He hoped he looked like someone looking for a friend.

Cedric wanted to explore the paddock, the saddling-up boxes, the race-course stables, the directors' room, the stewards' room, the commentary box, the judge's box, the weighing room, the jockeys' changing room. Dan tried to deter her from some of these, but she slipped away from him, wriggled through the crowd at knee level, and disappeared into the weighing room. The jockeys' room was beyond it. Dan waited by the unsaddling enclosure for Cedric to be ejected. He continued looking round for a big man, possibly now clean-shaven, almost certainly still with a stiff neck.

Cedric returned, her face pink with outrage.

'Throw you out, did they?' said Dan.

'Of course not. I said I was Lester Piggot's nephew.'

Dan nodded. He was continuing to underestimate Cedric.

'The jockeys were *dressing*,' Cedric whispered furiously.

'They're expected to,' said Dan.

'I mean, they were *un*dressing.'

'Necessary step,' said Dan. 'Can't do one without the other.'

'We must go and look at the horses.'

'Yes, but don't go forgetting what we're really here for.'

'Of course not,' said Cedric: but she had eyes for nothing but the horses.

A dozen were being led round the parade-ring for the first race, a selling hurdle. Cedric stared at them, wide-eyed, adoring. Each, as it passed them, was her confident selection to win this race and then to go on to win the Grand National. A small clump of colonels stood in the middle of the paddock: the

Stewards. Owners and trainers came in, and presently the jockeys, little leathery men and pale boys and tall, skinny amateurs. Cedric radiated hero-worship.

There was a Monday crowd round the paddock, a selling-hurdle crowd. It was possible to see every member of it. Cedric said she inspected every face, but Dan was not quite sure that this was true.

Their man might perfectly well not be bothering with the paddock for this race. He might be racing in the Silver Ring, without access to the paddock, or be on the other side of the race-course. He might perfectly well, come to that, have been carrying binoculars for some quite different reason. It was no good thinking on those lines.

Cedric settled on a horse called Sophie's Friend, a selection Dan found surprisingly sentimental. Sophie's Friend was a washy chestnut with bandaged forelegs, unplaced in four outings already, although the season was young. He was credited to a trainer Dan had never heard of, and ridden by a jockey who looked frightened. He was a rank outsider. Dan seldom bet, and without inside information of a kind he rarely received he would not have touched Sophie's Friend with a bargepole. He tried to argue Cedric out of backing this obscure no-hoper, but Cedric was adamant.

They queued together for the Tote. Dan had £1 each way on Sophie's Friend. He gave the tickets to Cedric.

'Mummy doesn't like betting,' said Cedric.

'Nor do I,' said Dan.

'I do.'

'We'll see if you still think so in ten minutes.'

Dan led Cedric up into the grandstand. Cedric produced a small dead animal from the front of her sweater which, unrolled, turned out to be a tweed cap. She put it on. It was a good deal too large, but it was a good idea. In her cap she looked more like a little boy at the races than any little boy at those races.

'Where did you come by that?' murmured Dan.

'Somebody gave it to me,' said Cedric, a lie rendered the more blatant by the wide innocence of her blue eyes.

Dan had to let it go. What with cars, bicycles, hats, and car-park badges, he had not been setting a good example.

He looked over the thin crowd in the grandstand. Cedric had eyes only for the horses, now cantering down to the start. The ground was soft; they were cutting in; divots flew from the horses' feet.

'They're off.'

Cedric gave a thin, taxi-horn peep of excitement. The horses came back, it seemed to Dan, scarcely faster than they had gone down. Cedric bounced and squeaked with excitement. In one sense she was a gratifying guest to bring to the races, very appreciative; she was not a single-minded collaborator in the search for a murderer.

Sophie's Friend won, to screams from Cedric and glum silence elsewhere. Two of the fancied horses had fallen and one was pulled up lame.

Dan thought there would be no bid for the winner at the auction after the race. But there was one: from Cedric. The horse was being led round and round in front of a small crowd. The auctioneer, on a flimsy little rostrum, invited bids with apparent insincerity. The winning trainer, evidently as surprised by his victory as everybody else, began to look relieved. Then Cedric suddenly bid £500.

'Five I'm bid, five hundred guineas,' said the auctioneer in tones of astonishment.

The trainer looked gloomy. He showed no sign of wanting to buy in his winner.

Dan, behind Cedric's back, gestured urgently at the auctioneer, who thought at first that he was bidding. For a sickening moment, Dan saw himself paying out 600 guineas for this dreadful horse: except that Cedric would probably top his bid. He shook his head violently at the auctioneer, and pointed downwards at Cedric. The auctioneer now understood who had made the bid. He looked as though he was feeling that everything was turning out exactly as he had expected.

'Seems there's been no bid for the winner,' said the auctioneer into his microphone.

'Yes there has!' said Cedric.

Dan made faces at the auctioneer, who was beginning to look rattled.

There was general laughter. All eyes were turned to Dan and Cedric. They had become extremely conspicuous. A few jolly men praised Cedric's sporting spirit. One advised Dan to take a leather to the lad.

'Don't you dare,' said Cedric to Dan.

Dan led her away to collect her winnings, which were over £40.

'I like the races,' said Cedric.

Dan dragged his collaborator into the other enclosures. They searched them briskly, because Cedric was in a hurry to get back to the paddock and the Tote.

The second race was a novice steeplechase.

'Follow a stable in form,' said Dan.

Cedric had other and more adventurous ideas. Her selection, on which she had £2 to win, pulled up after running out. Cedric said the jockey had cheated, which Dan thought possible but unlikely.

On the third race, the sponsored handicap 'chase, Cedric lost more of her winnings. She took it badly.

Dan was beginning to feel cold. He searched once again through Tatts and the Silver Ring, and looked in every bar. He began to list in his mind all the purposes for which a man might carry a pair of binoculars. He thought an antique dealer, or someone feasibly taken for an antique dealer, was highly likely to be a bird-watcher.

Just after the fourth race, on which she lost again, Cedric disappeared briefly. She reappeared to whisper to Dan, 'I've seen him!'

Her whisper was loud enough to be heard by a dozen people round them in the grandstand.

Cedric tugged at Dan's sleeve. He followed her toward the Members' Car-park, and towards the marquee of Messrs Blackmore.

'He went in there,' said Cedric.

The uniformed sentries were still by the door. Dan thought that the hat from the Volvo, in combination with his banker's suit and his day-badge for the Members', might get him past the sentries. He was quite wrong. They had strict orders to admit no one without an invitation from the brewery. As he argued, Dan tried to see past the sentries into the marquee. It was full of publicans and licensed grocers tanking up at the brewery's expense. There were a few beards, and a lot of people Dan could not see.

He said, in the tones of an amiable, a cajoling Captain of Marines, 'A bloke I want a word with has just gone in, I gather. Big fellow with a beard.'

'That's right, sir,' said one of the sentries. 'There's dozens of beavers in there. Funny how they're back in fashion. I never fancied a beard meself, an' I don't think the wife would, either. I'll 'ave to suggest you wait for your friend out here, sir, seein' I'm strickly forbidden to admit wi'out card of invitation.'

Cedric, under cover of this parley, disappeared into the tent. Dan waited. He waited for twenty minutes in the increasing cold. He dared not explain to the sentries that his nephew had vanished into the marquee. Cedric had drawn enough attention to herself already. There must now be a nationwide hunt for her, with Sylvia lashing the police into the most furious activity.

Cedric came out of the tent.

She said, 'They gave me a super tea. I said my father owned the pub in Stepleton Underhill. I had a coke and a bitter lemon and a pineapple juice and six different sorts of cake and a ham sandwich.'

'Is he still in there?'

'No. I looked everywhere.'

'You're certain you saw him go in?'

'Yes, of course. He must have come out again while I was fetching you.'

'Anyway we know he's here . . .'

'Yes, of course. I expect he's at the paddock. We'd better go and look.'

He was not at the paddock. He was not in Tatts or the Silver Ring, or in the infield, which was scrubby and almost empty. He was not in any bar or in the grandstand.

During this search Dan lost Cedric again. Suddenly anxious,

he hurried up and down the enclosures, looking for her as well as for the bearded man. She rejoined him by the paddock.

'I went to the place where the big lorries are,' said Cedric.

'Horse-boxes?'

'They were putting horses into some of them. They're going home to their stables, lucky things. Most of the horses were very good about going in. They went rattle-rattle up into the lorries. I saw him again.'

'Where?'

'Getting into one of the lorries. Into the front, with the driver.'

6

'My God,' said Dan.

'You mustn't say that. Mummy never lets me say it.'

'You're right. Did the – the lorry go off?'

'Yes, of course. It had a name.'

'One of the transport firms, I suppose,' said Dan, thinking with despair of the police work which now faced him.

'I don't know. In big letters on the back, at the top, it said "*Racehorses*".'

'I see how it might.'

'Then it said, "*C. J. Wykes*".'

'Christie Wykes,' said Dan. 'He's a trainer. Local. I saw he had some runners, but I didn't see him.'

'Do you know him?' said Cedric, awed.

'By name and sight.'

'That's nothing. *I* know the *Queen* by name and by sight.'

'Your man got into C. J. Wykes's box, and went away in it?'

'Yes.'

'Hum. Might have been cadging a lift. But not if he lives in Stepleton – Wykes is at Beeston, the other direction. Business with Wykes? Antiques? Selling antiques to Wykes's old lady? Lives at Beeston, just visiting Stepleton? Hell of a coincidence if so, him being there twice when you were there . . . Lives at Beeston but works in Stepleton? Connected with Wykes? Racehorse owner? Vet, farrier, feed-merchant, horse-dealer . . . Gum, there's an awful lot of possibilities.'

'We'll have to go and find out,' said Cedric.

'That's what we'll have to do.'

'I've never been to a training stable. Can I go round it? Can I ride a horse? Can I be a jockey?'

'I daresay,' said Dan. 'Let's get away now.'

'But there's one more race. We must stay and see it.'

'Better choice of vehicles if we leave before the last.'

'All right. That car was too small.'

Dan retrieved his knapsack from the cloakroom. It did nothing for his image. He overcompensated for it, perhaps, by strutting arrogantly into the Members' Car-park. At least his hat and Cedric's cap were all right.

It was legitimate to wander in an exploratory way among the cars. People often forgot where they had left their cars, especially if they arrived late and in a hurry. People who had been given lifts might forget what car to return to. The nearer they were to the exit, the quicker they would get away, the fewer people would see them driving. Dan steered Cedric away from a Rolls towards a 2-litre Renault with the key in the dash and some rugs in the back.

A few other people were leaving before the last. Dan gave them time to get to their cars, in case any of them were making for the Renault.

They waited another minute until they could hear, from the loudspeaker in the distance, that the last race had started. Everybody's attention would be more or less on the race.

The man on the gate gave them a perfunctory salute, to which Cedric responded with a Queen-Mother wave.

Dan found himself, as he drove, embarked once again on an utterly unplanned course of action. It would be evident folly not to go to Beeston and to Christie Wykes's stables; but he had no idea what to do when he got there.

There was a back way, fifteen miles of very narrow lanes; there was a longer way on bigger roads; it was half an hour either way. He took the back way. He would be there soon after five. Wykes had no runners in the last two races, so he'd be home before they got there. Doing what? Having his tea? Highly likely that owners would be visiting, when he had runners at his local meeting. Impossible to gatecrash a party like that. Impossible to get Wykes off on his own. Then there'd be 'evening stables', the ritual made more ritualistic for the owners. You could possibly tag on to that, once it was getting dark. Was there any point in that? Suppose their man was a stable-lad at

Wykes's? No – stable-lads were not all midgets, but most of them started by trying to be jockeys.

Again, again, the basic – *What sort of a man was he?* Not an antique dealer, anyway not at 'Ships and Sealingwax' in Stapleton. But Sylvia, it seemed from what Cedric said, had thought he was. She had tried to buy chairs from him. He was feasibly an antique dealer, then – as feasibly at least as Dan was a Captain of Marines. So not Wykes's farrier or feed-merchant – his vet possibly. An owner possibly. No – neither vets nor racehorse-owners rode bicycles to meet friends to get lifts to Igton races.

In confusion, in something like despair, Dan pictured a well-spoken but impoverished feed-merchant getting a lift to the races and a lift from the races . . . He had left in the box a little after four. The box would go the long way round, but it would be there before Dan was. The man would be out of the cab and – what? Away in a car, on a motorbike, indoors, up in a feed-store?

Maybe out of the cab long before the box reached Beeston. Maybe a lift of a mile or two, a few hundred yards. Maybe a mate of the box-driver, completely unknown to Christie Wykes.

The person they had to talk to was the box-driver. Maybe part-time or full-time. Maybe lived on the place or in the village or miles away. Must have a name. Must be known to Wykes, to his head lad, to all the stable-lads. In that job he must have a telephone.

'A penny for your thoughts,' said Cedric, a phrase she was more likely to have got from Julie than from her mother.

'Not worth it,' said Dan. 'Rubbish.'

Christie Wykes's training stables were a disappointment to both Dan and Cedric.

They arrived openly, as befitted their car and headgear. There were no owners. There was no trainer. There was no formal 'evening stables'. Christie Wykes was away in Ireland, said the head lad, looking at some unbroken three-year-olds in a field, with a talent-spotter from Wexford. His wife was in

Yorkshire, with their daughter, who was having a baby. He, the head lad, was in charge for the week. He was pretty busy. If Captain Maltravers wanted to send a horse to the governor, that was grand, but it was the governor he'd have to talk to.

The gigantic horse-box was parked just outside the stable yard. Dan asked about a man who had been given a lift, in the cab of the box, from Igton races. It was a highly peculiar question. Dan tried to make it natural, casual: but it sounded peculiar to his own ears, and the head lad thought it was peculiar.

'A bloke we're anxious to talk to,' said Dan, 'on a confidential matter. My son Cedric caught a glimpse of him.'

The head lad, who resembled a weatherbeaten leather shooting-boot, looked at Dan as though Dan was crazy. But he was obliged to humour a potential owner with a new imported car and an expensive furry felt hat.

'Harry drove the box,' he said. He raised his voice and shouted, 'Harry!'

A nondescript man in a knitted cap came out of a loosebox, carrying a bucket. He was evidently a stable-lad who doubled as box-driver. Wykes's was not a big training stable.

'What's this about you giving people lifts, then?' said the head lad to Harry. 'You know what the guv'nor says about that.'

Harry scratched his head under the knitted cap. He put down his bucket, and scratched his head with both hands. It occurred to Dan, as ridiculous thoughts do at moments of supreme crisis, that the woolly cap tickled Harry's scalp.

'I 'ad Blackie Blair in box wi' me,' said Harry at last.

'Goin', yes,' said the head lad. 'What price comin' back?'

Harry scratched his head with both hands and said, 'Comin' back, I 'ad Blackie Blair wi' me.'

Dan's heart was jumping. Blackie Blair. What manner of man? How connected with Piet Vandervelde? It was the moment of truth.

Dan glanced at Cedric. It was getting dark. Lights were switched on in the yard. The peak of Cedric's extensive cap cast a shadow over her sharp little face. Dan could not read her expression.

'Blackie Blair the bloke you want, sir?' said the head lad.

'Know when we see him,' said Dan, with difficulty.

'Blackie!' yelled the head lad.

The cry was taken up by half a dozen stable-lads who were feeding, watering, or mucking out.

Blackie Blair appeared. Dan stared at him blankly. He was a tiny, middle-aged Irishman. Dan knew him by sight, although he had never heard his name. He was Christie Wykes's travelling lad, who went to the races whenever the stable had a runner, to take charge of horses and tack and lads. He had saddled Wykes's runners that afternoon at Igton. Dan had watched him doing so. It was obvious that he was called Blackie because his hair was so pale that it was colourless. If he had grown a beard it would have been invisible.

Blackie Blair looked at Dan and Cedric with wonder and some impatience.

'Oi jost shtarted me tay,' he said.

'Must have been your other box,' said Dan to the head lad.

'Other box?' said the head lad. 'We only ran four. That box holds seven. We *got* no other box.'

It was an embarrassing moment. They all stood there in the gathering darkness, in the mouth of the stable yard, with a small group of stable-lads silent and curious in the pool of light in the opening, Dan staring at Blackie Blair, all of them staring at Dan. He felt his nob disguise stripped away by those knowing eyes.

With Blackie's connivance, Harry the box-driver must have given a lift to another man, against the stable rules. In front of the head lad, neither Blackie nor Harry would admit to breaking those rules. In public, here and now, there was no way Dan was going to get the name, address, or trade of the other passenger in the horse box: Blackie and Harry would deny, flatly, interminably, that there had ever been another passenger. That did not necessarily mean that they were in any way implicated with Cedric's man, it just meant they wanted to stay out of trouble with their boss. It was the word of one strange small boy against their combined words. Dan did not want trouble for Blackie or Harry. He did not want trouble for Cedric, or for himself. He wanted to know something – anything – about the man they had given a lift to.

Dan needed a word in private with the box-driver, or the travelling lad, or both. But not now.

'My son must have made a mistake,' said Dan.

'I didn't!' said Cedric.

'That's not our friend, son. That's Mr Blair.'

Cedric opened her mouth to say something. She shut it again. Presumably she saw the uselessness of persisting. She tugged at Dan's sleeve. Dan lowered his head so that Cedric could whisper in his ear.

'They're telling lies,' whispered Cedric. 'I *did* see him.'

Dan nodded, at the same time making a new plan.

To the head lad he said, 'Never mind about that. Some kind of misunderstanding. I'll call Mr Wykes next weekend when he's back from Ireland.'

'Very good, sir,' said the head lad. His expression said that this was a new owner the stable could do without.

Dan and Cedric started back to the car. The head lad, Harry, Blackie Blair and other men stood watching them in silence, all the way to the car. Harry had picked up his bucket, and was scratching his head with one hand only.

'We'll come and have a peep in the morning,' murmured Dan to Cedric as they got into the car.

'Yes,' said Cedric. 'Where are we going to have tea?'

Cedric wanted to stop at the pub in Beeston village. Dan thought this a bad idea. Wykes's stable-lads would use that pub. Blackie Blair might come; Harry the box-driver might come; but not alone, not liable to confide in front of their mates that they had broken the rules of the stable by giving an outsider a lift in the box.

Dan drove around until the car was almost out of petrol, looking for somewhere to eat and to stay. There were no filling stations open. The country was all strange to Dan, and there was no map in the car. The names on the signposts were unfamiliar. It was a country of steep little hills and blind corners. They found villages with pubs, but some of the pubs had no bedrooms and others had bedrooms that were occupied – people come for the races, perhaps. Nobody could think of a Bed and Breakfast open at the end of October. The Stepleton establishment seemed unique. Cedric mourned it, knowing that she could have had her breakfast in bed there.

They got some food in a pub called the Fox and Hounds, in a village to them nameless.

When she had finished eating – all but the last mouthful, which she was still eating – Cedric said, 'I'm going to ring up Julie. Do you want to talk to her?'

'If you talk to her, and then I talk to her, she'll know you're with me.'

'So she will,' said Cedric.

'In two minutes they'll all know, your mother and the police and everybody.'

'So they will.'

Dan felt unreasonably pleased at this small triumph.

'All the same, it might be a good idea, me talking to Julie,' said Dan. 'Her Dad might have told her what the bluebottles are thinking.'

Dan used a coin-box in a passage. He found himself talking to PC Gundry. He asked for Julie. He said, in a high, pedantic voice, that he was Dr Maltravers.

To Julie he said, in his ordinary voice, 'How are you, love?'

Julie gave a scream. She said she was alone and could talk. She said, 'Have you got Anna?'

'Who's Anna?' said Dan. Then remembering an epoch when Cedric had been so called, he said, 'She was at home when I left.'

Dan asked her what had been going on and what her father had been saying. It was extremely interesting.

Sylvia, Mrs Vandervelde, had reached the house of her friends in Kent early on Saturday afternoon. They were all there, Ralph Watts and his mother and sister and the husband for Sophie. In the evening Ralph Watts had left, in his car, saying he had an appointment. He was meeting a man to talk about shooting rights. He said he would be back. He wasn't back. He hadn't come back and he still wasn't back, and there was no trace of his car.

'He was after Mrs V.,' said Julie.

'He was that,' said Dan.

'Well, the police know that. And of course they know *he* knew Sophie wasn't at home on Saturday night.'

'Gabby bloke, your Dad,' said Dan. 'He ought to be ashamed, telling you all this.'

'Everybody knows it. Everybody knows Mr Watts is after Mrs V., and everybody knew all along he gave her Sophie, and now everybody knows Sophie was away on Saturday night, and everybody knows where she went. Village are dreadful, really, aren't they?'

'Seethen wi' salacious mutterens,' said Dan, in one of his voices.

'Everybody's been told to look out for the car and to look out for Ralph Watts. And of course they're all hunting for Anna. A lot of people think Ralph Watts has got Anna, but I don't quite see why he should want her. Some people think you've got her. You shouldn't have left your cycle where you did.'

'Bicycle,' said Dan absently, having been put right by Cedric about this usage.

'I said I didn't see you,' said Julie, 'so they think you came to steal things. They'd like to think Mr V. caught you at it, and you shot him.'

'Neat scenario,' said Dan. 'But I don't look like the bloke Cedric saw.'

'Who's Cedric?'

'I mean Anna.'

Julie suddenly began to talk about wages and hours of work, and called him Doctor, by which Dan understood that she was no longer alone.

There were sounds of movement at Julie's end, a door closing, and a change in Julie's voice.

She said, 'Old Cyril Bliss came to see Dad today.'

'Blinky?' said Dan. 'I saw him, night before last. Shocking, the effects of ardent spirits.'

'He wasn't drunk. He was blind.'

'Blind drunk?'

'No, he'd lost his spectacles. He was spending a penny in the woods on the way home from the pub, and a twig pulled his glasses off, and he couldn't find them.'

'Gum,' said Dan, remembering the exhausting bicycle sprint which was now shown to have been needless.

'He saw a car in the woods, near the Old Hall, with a man in it. As soon as he heard about the murder he came to tell Dad.'

'Right public-spirited.'

'So the man Anna saw has a car.'

'Or borrowed one, or nicked one. What kind of a car?'

'Cyril Bliss doesn't know. Just a pale-coloured car. He's really blind without his glasses. A man in the car, but he couldn't see him either.'

'That's a fat lot of help, then.'

'Well, it proves somebody else *was* about the place, as well as you.'

'It might have been Piet Vandervelde, on his way *to* the house.'

'No, his car was a hired black Mercedes. They found that straight away.'

Julie began gabbling about the payment of her return fare to Saudi Arabia.

'Let us have your decision at your earliest convenience,' said Dan, in the tones of Dr Maltravers.

He hung up and returned to Cedric, who took over the coin-box to call his mother.

'I told her I was all right,' said Cedric, herself returning after an unexpectedly long time away from food. 'I told her not to worry. She said, "Are you with Dan Mallett?" I said, "Who's Dan Mallett?" She said, "Are you with Uncle Ralph?" I said no. She said she'd been trying to get hold of Uncle Ralph, but he's gone away and she's lost the bit of paper with his special telephone number. I said I was still with three ladies.'

'Three. Used to be only one.'

'I said three. They'll be looking for three ladies with a little girl. I said what the ladies looked like.'

'What do they look like?'

'One very fat and one very thin and one bald.'

'A bald lady?'

'With a wig. A red wig, I said. They'll be looking for a lady with a red wig.'

Cedric recommenced his meal, or began another, for which Dan was asked to pay. Watching her eat – watching her take full advantage of the relaxation of the rules about eating to which she was normally subject – Dan tried to ponder the implications of all he had learned.

Of all the people who had motives for killing Piet Vandervelde, Ralph Watts had as strong a motive as any. He was barmy about Sylvia. He could have told Piet, in some roundabout way, that Anna was going to be at home on Saturday night, when Sylvia and the dog would be away. Perhaps he had pinched a latchkey; perhaps Sylvia had given him one. He had sat in the hall, waiting for Piet, knowing Piet would come to get his child. He then nipped away, ran to the car he'd left hidden somewhere, and left Dan to take the rap. Not knowing Dan was there, but assuming a burglar or burglars unknown would take the rap. Fine, fine, except that Ralph Watts was a slight, fair man, not much bigger than Dan, a wiry little man who rode in point-to-point races. It was possible he might get a boil on his neck, but in all other ways he was simply not the man Cedric saw.

Ah! He had *hired* the man Cedric saw. He had made the arrangement, probably, as soon as he knew Sylvia was bringing the dog to Kent.

Then where had he gone on Saturday night, and where was he now, and why? Sitting at home, with his family and Sylvia, he would have had a perfect alibi. Suppose he had gone along to make sure all went well? Suppose he had been at Medwell Old Hall? Suppose he had fixed himself an alibi, say with a tart? Suppose he had wanted to see for himself that Piet was well and truly blasted, but he hadn't wanted to do the blasting? That was possible. On balance, it seemed the most likely. But where was he now? Why?

It was as necessary as ever to find Cedric's man, and the place to start looking was Christie Wykes's stable-yard. Not that the man would be there, but one or two stable-lads almost certainly knew who he was.

The profile of the man, as revised by all this, blurred and reformed. He was a gunman, a hired killer, who seemed to Sylvia like an antique dealer, who rode a bicycle in the Stepleton village street, who went to Igton races, and cadged a lift in a horse-box. He was big and fat, and had a beard and a boil.

He sounded a horrible man. Dan was alarmed at the thought of meeting him, of denouncing him to the police. A man like that had mates, horrible underworld heavies who avenged their friends with razors in alleyways. Dan thought he could avoid any gangsters he had a mind to avoid, but what about Cedric?

He thought he must be overtired and overstrained, to be thinking in these ghoulish terms.

He bought cheese rolls, cold sausages, and Pepsi-Cola from the pub, for their breakfast.

They slept in the car. It was cold. Dan wore his country clothes over his banker's clothes, and Cedric had the two rugs. Dan set his mental alarm to get them up at dawn. Blackie Blair and Harry would almost certainly be riding work, with the first lot, on the gallops. It might be possible to talk to one or other of them privately: and if not then, later.

Dan duly woke to see a glow of cold, butter-coloured light in the east. Cedric was still asleep, cocooned in the rugs on the back seat. Her cropped yellow hair stood on end. Asleep, she looked very young and vulnerable. Dan felt aghast at what he was subjecting her to, until he remembered that she was doing the subjecting.

Cedric woke in holiday spirits. She was cock-a-hoop at having been to the races for the first time in her life, and at having stood in the actual yard of an actual training stable talking to actual stable-lads. She said she would be a stable-lad when she was grown up, in fact long before that, as well as a jet pilot and pop singer and Member of Parliament.

She said the sausages and Pepsi were the best breakfast she had ever eaten. She was never allowed Pepsi at home. She said she never wanted to go home or back to school; she wanted to spend her life with Dan driving borrowed cars and doing exciting things and eating sausages.

Dan buried the greasy bits of paper which had protected the sausages from Cedric during the night, digging a hole in a drift of rotting leaves with the jack-handle of the car In doing so, he disturbed a small parcel of field-voles who had made a nest for the winter under the natural compost-heap in the wood. Cedric was fascinated by the voles. She noticed, unprompted, that they were much burlier than mice, with blunt noses instead of sharp ones, short tails instead of long ones, little ears instead of big ones. They were reddish-brown, a prettier colour than mice. Their whiskers alone were completely mouselike. Cedric wanted to catch one, keep it as a pet, and call it Dan. Dan, though touched, said it would be cruel because the other voles would miss Dan, and pine away and sicken.

Holly-berries and yew-berries spangled with pillar-box red the dark green of their trees. There was no other bright colour anywhere. But there were gentle colours, colours of winter, visible as the sun hooked an eyebrow over the hills to the east. On the rough bark of the trees of the wood, a film of new green was appearing – moss, dormant all summer, now revived in the cool and damp of autumn: a curious, comfortable, useless plant obeying rules opposite to those of other plants which slept in winter and flourished in summer. High in the same trees a few leaves still hung, forming in the dawn a golden mist caught in the tracery of bare twigs, as though blown there and trapped. Robins were busy and noisy. A wren approached the car, singing lustily as though he thought it was spring, his song impossibly loud from so small a bird. He quivered with the song; he looked about to burst. He was not shy but he was not sociable, like the robins. He was not interested in people, but in his own concerns which preoccupied him completely. He was very busy and in a hurry. He went on his way, still singing.

Cedric looked after him with a regret which Dan shared. Cedric said, 'Is that a boy or girl?'

'No way of knowing,' said Dan.

'There must be. Boys and girls are always different.'

'Not wrens. Not redbreasts, either.'

'They must be different. Or how do *they* know? If they weren't different, a boy might marry a boy and a girl might marry a girl.'

'Daresay they can tell,' said Dan.

'If they can, you ought to be able to,' said Cedric.

It was evident to Dan that he had sunk, once again, in Cedric's regard. Any points he had scored were lost.

It was still very early when they set off for Beeston. Dan went gingerly, looking at the pessimistic needle of the petrol-gauge. There'd be no all-night garages on these lanes, and the others wouldn't be open for two hours. In a maze of little hills and unfamiliar place-names, he tried to steer by the sun, but the lanes refused to co-operate and took them in whimsical directions. They came to a main road. Petrol was now more likely; so was a police car with the number of the Renault. The chance had to be taken.

Dan turned on to the main road. To Cedric's annoyance he drove slowly, husbanding his spoonfuls of petrol. The gauge had said zero for a long time. There was no traffic; ordinary people were not yet up, except in training stables.

They passed two filling stations, both closed.

The engine began to cough apologetically. There were gaps between deliveries of petrol to the carburettor.

'What a rotten car,' said Cedric.

Ahead, visible from a long way off, was a bright Esso sign. Below the oval Dan read, 'Open 24 hours'. The engine died. They coasted, soundlessly except for the whisper of wheels on the tarmac, and came to a halt five hundred yards from the garage.

'Bit o' luck,' said Dan. 'They'll have a can. You coming or staying?'

'I'll stay,' said Cedric.

Dan got out of the car and began walking. He still had his

country clothes over his banker's clothes. He was glad, for it was a chilly morning.

After a few moments Cedric came trotting after him.

A police car came towards them, from the south, fast. It slowed by the garage, began to accelerate, screeched to a stop by the Renault.

'My God, I mean my golly,' said Dan. 'Keep walking. It's a good job you came with me after all.'

'Yes, I know,' said Cedric predictably. 'That's why I came, in case the police saw the car.'

'Something I should have thought of,' said Dan.

'Yes, I know. But it doesn't matter, because I thought of it.'

It was natural to look at the policemen. Dan did so, over his shoulder, as he walked. He did not know where he was walking to. It was enough to be increasing the distance between them and the bluebottles.

One policeman had got into the unlocked Renault. Dan's knapsack was there. Toothbrush, razor and so forth. Clean socks. Nothing marked, all anonymous, the knapsack itself an unwitting present from a gamekeeper. Cedric's tweed cap was in the car, and the felt hat from the Stepleton Volvo. They could probably be traced, but not to Cedric and Dan.

The other policeman was using his radio.

A fold in the ground hid the scene for a moment. Cedric and Dan were almost on the garage's forecourt. The sun was clear of the horizon, revealing the dirt on Cedric's face.

An engine hummed. The police car was beside them. Dan wanted to run away, very fast, in any direction, which would have been a thoroughly bad idea.

7

'Is that your car?'

'Which one?' said Dan, playing for time.

The police car had stopped. The man beside the driver, his window down, pointed back down the road to the stranded Renault.

Dan greatly disliked being inspected at close range by beady-eyed bluebottles, their faces bright with suspicion. He was thankful to be far from home. Policemen from anywhere near Medwell would have recognized him.

Dan regretted that he was still wearing his poaching clothes over his banking clothes. He was not Captain Maltravers, RM. It was no good pretending to be that sort of nob or any other sort of nob. He imagined he looked pretty strange, bulky and misshapen as well as scruffy.

Adopting an accent to match his outer garments, Dan said, at his most treacly, 'Nay. We ben hitchen. A-ben an ol' lorry did brung we t'thicky spot.'

'We ben hitchen t'Maister Wykes, yonder t'Beeston,' said Cedric, wide-eyed, impossible to disbelieve.

'Ay,' said Dan, grateful for the lead, but careful not to show this to Cedric. 'A-did heard there were mebbe a job yonder t'Wykes. A-ben kin t'stable-lad. A-do onnerstand they gee-gees.'

'Mm,' said the policeman. 'What's that laddie doing, traipsing round the country? Why isn't he at school?'

'A-will be t'larnen, better nor I ever,' said Dan earnestly, expressing with lowered eyes his reverence for education. 'Soon's a-do fix meself up wi' job.'

'Me Mam done a bunk,' said Cedric plaintively. 'Lef' we t'muddles.'

'Tes true,' said Dan, trying to subdue the exuberance of Cedric's imagination with a ferocious glance. Cedric looked as much like a cherub as her sharp urchin features permitted. She was unsubdued. She was pleased with her contribution to the interview.

Facing the realities of the ridiculous situation Cedric had created, Dan assumed the expression of a wronged and deserted husband, learned from a number of husbands of his acquaintance.

'Done a bunk wi' a travellen gent,' he said.

'You're going the wrong way for Beeston,' said the policeman.

'Ay,' said Dan. 'But thicky spot d'seem a grand place for t'hitch, wi' cars astoppen an' astarten. Mebbe somebody gi' we a hitch t'Beeston, after a-done drinken up thicky fire-juice.'

'Fire-juice' was a gross, a ludicrous extravagance. Dan could have kicked himself for falling into the trap of grievous self-parody, as he so often did but seldom at moments so critical.

'Hm,' said the policeman, a sound full of menace. 'You've just walked past that car?'

'Ay,' said Dan anxiously. 'Warn't no good fer no hitchen, see, 'cos driver ben an' left un.'

'Did you see the driver?'

'Nay!'

'I saw the driver,' said Cedric, for a moment incautious as to accent.

'Nay, ye never!' said Dan.

'A-dun,' said Cedric, recollecting her role. 'Big bloke, a-was, wi' a beard like a billy-goat.'

There was a visible reaction from the policemen in the car. That meant that they were looking for a big man with a beard. That meant that they believed Julie's account of Anna's description of the murderer: or at least that they took it seriously. Of course they were also looking for Anna, in the company of female kidnappers one of whom had a red wig. There was not much chance of their recognizing a rich little girl, very strictly brought up, in the grubby urchin with sticking-out ears who spoke (with occasional lapses) in broad stage Loamshire.

And of course they were looking for Dan, on account of the incriminating bicycle, and because he had disappeared, and because he was the biggest villain unhung. They were looking for Dan alone, not for a stable-lad with a small boy. Cedric was a kind of camouflage.

'Where did the bloke go?' asked the nearest policeman.

Cedric pointed vaguely at the steep little hills through which the road ran.

The police driver began to talk urgently to his radio. Soon the place would be buzzing with bluebottles. Dan was not sure Cedric's idea had been a good one. Cedric's expression showed that she was quite sure it was a very good one.

Maybe she thought it would shift attention from themselves. Maybe she thought it would shift attention to herself. Maybe, in a funny way, a bit of both.

'How was it you never saw the bloke?' said the policeman to Dan, while his mate was furiously summoning reserves by the radio.

'Warn't looken,' said Dan apologetically.

'Kid done better than his Dad.'

'Yes, of course,' said Cedric, again forgetting her accent. 'Sart'nlee,' she added.

They got a lift in a police car to Beeston, after no trace had been found of a large bearded man in the stretch of rough country into which Cedric had said he had disappeared. They were given the lift because of their help to the police: Cedric's help to the police. The thanks of the police were, under the circumstances, addressed more especially to Cedric. Cedric was inclined to smirk. Dan was deeply uneasy, sitting in the back of a police car with Cedric. Cedric enjoyed the drive, although she began to complain of hunger.

The two policemen in the front of the car were very chatty. They drew Cedric out. They were avuncular. They showed a side of the force not previously vouchsafed to Dan. Cedric gave a lurid account of her early childhood, of a degree of maternal cruelty which it would have interested Sylvia to hear. Cedric was clever about it. She described her own life, but transferred it to George and Dorothy Barrow's cottage in the Old Hall garden. It all rang true, and was a tale to wring tears from a statue. The policemen lapped it up. Dan was half ashamed of Cedric, and half proud of her.

Cedric was thoroughly ashamed of Dan, for being unshaven and nervous in the back of a police car.

'Where's your baggage? Your things? Clothes? Kit?' the policeman beside the driver suddenly asked, looking at Cedric over his shoulder.

Cedric glanced helplessly at Dan, who felt as helpless as she looked.

'In store, like,' said Dan. 'Over t'the ol' 'oman's. She ben especken for we t'colleck un when we's set.'

'What old woman?'

What old woman?

'Ben call Miss Grimthorpe,' said Dan, pulling this name out of some unidentified socket in his memory.

Cedric giggled. 'Got purple on her face,' said Cedric.

Dan remembered that Miss Grimthorpe's marble portrait bust was the reason Cedric was here. The name would do, as well as another. The policeman seemed satisfied by this enigmatic explanation. Dan felt, not for the first time, that he had long lost touch with the sane and predictable world.

The police car dropped them in Beeston village at about eleven. Dan felt peculiar, climbing out of a police car like a council official or even a detective, under the eyes of a busy village. Cedric descended like a royal bridesmaid.

Just as the police car drove away, Dan found himself thinking again about fingerprints. The Renault was stolen and known to be stolen. The word 'borrowed' would impress nobody. The police seemed to think it possible that the thief (not feasibly to be called the 'borrower') was the murderer of Piet Vandervelde, owing to Cedric's improvisation. They would therefore fingerprint the steering-wheel before anybody touched it. No doubt they had long ago done so. Probably Dan could have watched them doing so while he and Cedric had waited for a lift at the garage. All over the steering-wheel they would find Dan's fingerprints. These police would say to other police, 'These are the fingerprints of a car-thief who might be the murderer you're looking for, who's a big bloke with a beard.' Probably they had some kind of central computer. The computer would be shown the fingerprints from the Renault. The computer would say to these police, 'No, mates, these are not the prints of any big bloke with or without a beard. These prints belong to Dan Mallett, biggest villain unhung, the one who left his bike outside the house where Piet Vandervelde was done in; a little bloke with blue eyes and mousey hair, currently on the run and suspected of practically everything.'

Dan wondered how long the computer would take to deliver this message, once the fingerprints were shown to it. He imagined about three seconds. He wondered how long it would take for the message to get out to all the cars. He imagined another three seconds. He regretted his ignorance of modern police procedures, regretted leaving his fingerprints all over the Renault, regretted having given in to Cedric's blackmail, regretted the years in prison which, it seemed to him, he undoubtedly faced.

The thing to do was to stay out of sight of all policemen and practically everybody else. The other thing to do was to find Christie Wykes's gallops, see his second or third lot working, and get hold, in a tactful way, of Harry the box-driver or Blackie Blair the travelling lad. It was probably impossible, though it had seemed easy, the night before. But it was absolutely the only thing Dan could think of – the only way to find out something about the man Cedric had seen.

It was astonishing the message had not come through to their police car, while they were in it, about the fingerprints and about Dan. It was the one good thing about a situation otherwise odious.

Dan went into a post office. He expected to see posters of himself – 'WANTED, *Alive or Dead, £1,000,000 Reward*' – but saw an old woman with a goitre behind the counter. She claimed to know where Christie Wykes's gallops were, but was unskilled in giving directions. Other persons in the post office helped. Dan emerged confused, and looked round for Cedric. Cedric had disappeared. Dan had a sudden urge to disappear too, to escape from his peonage; but it remained true that Cedric was the only person who could positively identify her father's murderer. Also Dan felt a certain responsibility for Cedric. He waited, fairly certain that Cedric would return, telling himself that Cedric felt a certain responsibility for him, and that Cedric could not drive a car, and that Cedric would shortly be hungry, and that the purple dye was still all over Cedric's forearm.

Dan saw Cedric in the place where he should immediately have looked for her, in the telephone box outside the post office. He made faces at her through the glass, pointing at an imaginary wrist-watch. She waved him away. She was talking earnestly, almost passionately, but too softly for Dan to hear. When she was not talking she was listening intently. She listened far more intently to the telephone than she ever did to Dan. She put another coin into the box. She looked like a very serious little boy discussing something of supreme importance, like the county cricket championship, or birds' eggs, or stamps.

At long last Cedric finished her call. Dan stepped forward to open the door of the telephone box. Cedric waved him away, at her most imperious, got out another 10-pence piece, and dialled again. She dialled without looking at a book or a piece of paper. It was a number she knew, probably her home. Now she was visibly talking to her mother. Her manner was completely different. All the high seriousness, the concentration, had gone. She was airy, debonair. She gestured widely as she talked. She was telling a pack of lies, another pack of lies, about women with red wigs and God knew what else.

The second call was much quicker than the first. She did not have much to say to her mother, and she hardly listened at all. She hung up after a final lie, and came out of the telephone box looking deeply pleased with herself.

'Who was that you were talking to?' asked Dan.

'Mummy.'

'Yes, but before that?'

'Oh, before that. I was talking to Lucinda Hanbury. She's my best friend at school. I said I was her aunt with an urgent private family message, so they went and fetched her out of prayers. I told her to feed my guinea-pigs. I keep them at school in the term-time, because I'm there more than I'm at home.

Lots of people have rabbits or guinea-pigs or hamsters. My guinea-pigs are called Nicholas and Tiggy. Lucinda has a rabbit called Uncle Giles. She turned out to be a girl, but Lucinda still calls her Uncle Giles. Anyway, that's all fixed. And Lucinda was telling me about the fuss over the purple paint on Miss Grimthorpe.'

'There is a fuss?'

'Yes, of course. And then I talked to Mummy. I told her not to worry and not to look for me.'

'What else did you tell her?'

'Nothing much. Just things to make her feel better. And a few things to make it more difficult for anybody to catch us.'

'Like red wigs?'

'Yes, and I said I was in Warwickshire.'

'Hum,' said Dan, startled. 'Why Warwickshire?'

'So they'll be looking for me in Warwickshire.'

'Yes, but why *Warwickshire?*'

'Because Lieutenant Cedric Maltravers comes from Warwickshire, of course.'

'Of course.'

'Now we'll go and see the horses galloping.'

'It's men we want to see.'

'Yes, we can look for them too.'

Dan was again dubious about Cedric's single-mindedness.

They set off on foot, in what Dan hoped was the right direction. After a mile they saw a sign warning motorists to watch out for racehorses. They were getting warm. Dan was getting very warm, and fed up with the absurd bulk of his double set of clothes. He went behind a hedge, took off his working clothes, then the banker's clothes he had on underneath, then resumed his ordinary clothes. He rolled up his smart suit carefully, and tied his tie round the bundle. He was now a more normal shape and a more normal temperature. Cedric was impatient with the delay.

'You kept me waiting a sight longer than that,' said Dan. 'All that phoning. Telephoning.'

'That was a matter of life or death,' said Cedric.

'Whose?'

'Nicholas and Tiggy's.'

'This is a matter of life or death, too. Mine.'

Three horses came towards them along the road, walking. The riders wore crash helmets. One rider was quite old, one a teen-aged boy, one a girl. The horses had rugs over their quarters: racehorses. One was blowing hard after his gallop. Dan guessed that the others had only cantered. Dan recognized none of the three riders; none was Harry the box-driver or Blackie Blair. But any of the three might have seen himself and Cedric the previous evening in the stable yard, under the bright light.

'Marnen,' said Dan as the leading rider passed them, fitting his speech to his garb.

The rider, the older man, looked at him with recognition and astonishment. He *had* seen Dan and Cedric in the stable, then. Dan remembered that he had been, at that awkward interview, a Marine captain in a smart dark suit with a Bond Street hat and an accent more or less to match.

'Nice clear morning,' said Dan, being Captain Maltravers.

The elderly stable lad continued to gape at him. He rode on by without saying anything.

'Blackie Blair ben still along t'gallops?' Dan asked the teen-aged boy, who came next. He was taking the chance that the boy had not seen them, would not recognize them.

The boy, with an apathetic face, made a noise like 'Ur'. In tone it could perfectly well have been 'yes' or 'no', or 'look out', or 'mind your own business', or 'I'm not allowed to say'. The boy rode on by.

Dan tried his smile on the girl, his best smile; the one he had used when Julie came along in the night with her bicycle; the one that had, long before, pacified Sylvia in her grandfather's garage. She smiled back. Dan's hopes rose. The girl would tell them what they wanted to know.

Before Dan had a chance to speak – while, indeed, he was still trying to decide what voice to use in this ambiguous situation – she said, 'You're the bloke got Harry into trouble. I wouldn't show my face if I was you. The boss'll fine him when he gets back from Ireland. He says he never gave nobody no lift in the box. He says he knows the rule and he knows the reason and he knows the boss, and he never gave no lift to nobody. I'd keep well clear of Harry if I was you. Boiling mad he is. I couldn't repeat what he said about you, not in front of the kid. But I'll tell you this much . . .'

By this time she had passed them, walking her horse back to the stables, and her words became indistinct and then inaudible. From the appearance of her back, Dan received the impression that she was still talking about the things Harry would do to Dan if he saw him.

Cedric said, 'Why aren't they allowed to give people lifts in the lorry?'

'Security,' said Dan. 'Risk o' the horses being got at.'

'How could you get at a horse if it's in the back and you're in the front?'

'Gas,' suggested Dan vaguely.

'Anyway he *did* give the man a lift. I *saw* the man get into the front of the lorry. They must be a gang, like Al Capo-Caponone. I expect they all pack rods.'

'Then we'd best go careful,' said Dan, not really frightened of Harry the driver but not wishing to face an infuriated man riding a ton of thoroughbred. The business of the rule, of Harry's fine, of Harry's rage, was distinctly inconvenient. It complicated a situation already fraught. It limited their quarry to Blackie Blair, Harry's superior. But Blackie Blair was equally guilty of breaking the stable rules. Presumably he would be fined too, and presumably, then, would be as angry as Harry. Nothing would be got out of either of them, and Dan was as far away as ever from locating Cedric's man.

The attempt had to be made. They walked on, Cedric excited at the prospect of watching the horses galloping. She was not frightened of a shoot-out with an armed gang.

Dan realized that they had passed a little road which was the back way to the stables. In some ways, he thought, it must be a nuisance having the gallops away from the stables, but on balance it was probably a good thing. The horses were walked out from their beds to the gallops, which got their circulation going and their muscles loosened; and they walked back after working, so that they cooled down naturally. Dan had heard that American trainers hitched their horses to a sort of powered towel-rail, which walked them round and round on the spot. Next thing they'd be galloping their horses on a conveyor-belt. He wondered if you could clock a horse on a treadmill, if you knew exactly what speed it was going . . . He tore his mind away from these profitless speculations to the problems and hazards of the present.

A gate stood open on to an unmade track which ran beside a small plantation of fir-trees to another gate in a high bullfinch hedge. A sign on the first gate said 'PRIVATE', but the message seemed to Dan to be cancelled by the gate's being open. He saw horses walking round in the field beyond the second gate.

'This is it,' said Dan.

Cedric looked as though she had expected something quite different and much more glamorous.

They went along the track beside the young firs.

'If they start coming through that gate, nip into the trees and hide,' said Dan

'Why?'

'There's hostile emotions,' said Dan. 'A grudging spirit.'

Three more horses started through the further gateway, and Dan and Cedric were instantly in the sketchy cover of the fir-trees. The horses walked away from the gallops in single file. Harry the box-driver was one of the riders, his woolly cap pulled down over his mandatory crash-helmet. Cedric squeaked at the sight of him, but Dan shushed her.

When the horses had gone out on to the road, they emerged from the plantation and went on, softly, alert.

Christie Wykes's gallops were much as Dan expected for a remote and fairly modest National Hunt stable: simply a couple of fields with the fence between taken away and the ditch filled. There was a fair slope, so the horses could do extra work galloping uphill and learn to gallop downhill. To travel more than about six furlongs, they had to go round the edge. Branches from the fir-trees were stuck into the ground to mark the strip they were using. There was no all-weather track of tan or sand. There were no schooling jumps – they must have had those in a paddock nearer the stables. The grass was grazed, not mown. Probably Christie Wykes fattened bullocks. Possibly he rented the fields, and the owner grazed them.

Half a dozen horses were circling, at a walk, at the far end of the modest tract of turf. Near the middle, on a pony, the head lad waited. Two of the horses detached themselves from the circling ring, and stood side by side. The head lad raised a hand with a fluttering handkerchief. He dropped it. The horses pounded side by side round the edge of the area, going a moderate gallop for three-quarters of a mile and then flat out for a few hundred yards, finishing up the hill. They pulled up opposite the head lad, the horses visibly steaming and sweating. No doubt the stable-lads riding them had been told exactly what to do and had done it. It was all pretty humdrum and thoroughly professional, as far as Dan could judge. As long as the weather held, you could get a Derby winner fit in a couple of fields like this: and as long as you gave them the right food and the right amount of work. Dan wondered what they did give thoroughbreds; his whole equine experience was with ponies. He had an idea there were all kinds of fancy vitamins . . . He pulled his mind back to business, peeping through the bullfinch hedge at the scene.

A very small man was riding one of the four horses left at the far end. Dan was sure this was Blackie Blair, though he was too far away to recognize. As number two to the head lad, he would have the job of sending the horses off, probably using a list the head lad had given him. If the trainer were here, the head lad would be doing that. Therefore Blackie Blair would be the last one to go. He might leave the place last, after the head lad. It was the thing to hope for.

The two horses which had just galloped had rugs thrown over their quarters. They walked towards the gate, and through it and away.

Cedric stared with love and longing at the horses.

Three of the remaining horses worked together, with a more sustained sprint at the end, passing close to the point where Dan and Cedric were ensconced in the bullfinch. Twelve iron-shod feet pounded by on the resilient turf. The lads crouched over their horses' necks, riding as short as proper jockeys but in a motley lot of clothes. Two of them wore jeans. None had riding boots. Sartorially they were midway between Dan and Cedric, except for their crash-helmets.

Cedric bounced with excitement as the horses went by. Dan thought that, except for the arrogance with which she would treat trainer and owners, she might make a good stable-girl. Even a jockey. She looked like an apprentice jockey, a sharp-faced boy with bat ears.

The tiny rider Dan assumed to be Blackie Blair trotted his horse towards the head lad's pony. He was not working his horse but only using it as a hack. Maybe it was retired, or recovering from a strained back, or simply being given a rest.

Horse and pony started together towards the gate. Dan wondered how Blackie Blair was going to react to seeing him. He wondered what the head lad would make of his changed appearance. He wondered what voice to use.

As he was wondering, Cedric said suddenly, 'Wait here.'

She scrambled through the overgrown hedge and ran towards the oncoming riders. They reined in. Dan heard voices coming down the slight breeze, but not what was said.

He admitted to himself that Cedric's idea was a good one, as long as she remembered to ask the one supremely important question, and remembered the answer. Dan did not think Blackie Blair would vent his rage on a skinny little boy.

The conversation went on for a long time. Dan thought Cedric was pleading. The whole aspect of her body and of her flapping hands expressed passionate appeal. She was begging for the name and address of the fat bearded man with a boil on his neck.

To Dan's surprise, both horsemen dismounted, and Blackie Blair held the heads of both horses. The head lad was beside Blackie Blair's horse, the thoroughbred, with Cedric, both hidden by the pony. Dan's surprise intensified into incredulous astonishment when he saw the head lad flip Cedric up into the thoroughbred's saddle. She sat as straight as a guardsman, and put her feet in the stirrups. The head lad took the pony's bridle, and Blackie Blair led Cedric round on the thoroughbred. They stopped after a twenty-yard circle. More pleading went on, but this time Cedric lost. The head lad, his pony's reins looped over his arm, lifted Cedric off the horse and deposited her on the ground. She shook hands with him and with Blackie Blair. The head lad gave Blackie Blair a leg up, mounted his own pony, and they walked to the gate. Cedric stood in the middle of the field, watching them go, in a rapturous trance. She seemed to be surrounded by an aura of worship.

She shook herself, like a dog, and trotted back to Dan's hiding place.

'Well?' said Dan.

'He's called Quintus,' she said. 'He's got a bad foot.'

'As well as a boil on his neck?'

'I don't think there's anything wrong with his neck. Isn't he *beautiful*?'

Dan understood that Quintus was the name of the horse, not of the bearded man.

He said, 'You did ask about the bloke they gave a lift to?'

'Yes, *of course*,' said Cedric. 'That's one of the reasons we came here. Mr Blair doesn't know the man's name, but he knows where he works. He works in the swimming-baths at Madwick.'

'Oh. Grand. Does he live in Madwick?'

'Mr Blair doesn't know where he lives. Just that he works in the swimming-baths.'

'Why did he want a lift to Beeston?'

'He lost all his money at the races. He went to see his old auntie, who lives in Beeston and is dying of leprosy.'

'I doubt it.'

'P'raps it was a different thing. Anyway she's *very* ill. That's why they gave the man a lift. So they've been forgiven.'

It was all perfectly feasible. A swimming-pool attendant could be a hired murderer, Dan supposed, as well as anybody else. He could be mistaken for somebody selling chairs in an antique shop. The bicycle he had ridden through Stepleton fitted that station in life, and Stepleton was not impossibly far from Madwick. The coincidence of Cedric seeing him twice in Stepleton was the only real oddity, and that oddity disappeared if he lived in Stepleton and only worked in Madwick.

'So we must have lunch and then go to the swimming-baths,' said Cedric.

This *must* be the end of the road, thought Dan. With luck he could be home by nightfall. He thought with passionate nostalgia of his snug little cottage, his dogs and birds and well-stocked larder. He thought with joy of being his own master again.

'Come on,' said Cedric. 'I'm hungry.'

8

They had lunch at a pub on the edge of Beeston village. Dan kept an eye out for any of Christie Wykes's employees, and especially for Harry the box-driver.

Cedric said, 'I think you ought to ring up Julie again.'

'Why?'

'All sorts of things have probably happened. They might have found the fat man.'

Dan doubted if Julie would have any more news for him, but 10 pence was a small price to pay for peace.

It was a small price to pay for the very hot news which, as it happened, Julie did have for him. Ralph Watts had reappeared. He had knocked on the door of the Medwell Fratrorum police station, and Julie herself had let him in. She said she let in a small, fair man, strange to her, and he had said he was Ralph Watts, and she'd nearly had a fit. She'd got her Dad out of the Chestnut Horse, and Ralph Watts had told his story. Julie heard the whole thing through the door. Then her Dad phoned Milchester, and more policemen came in a car, and they took Ralph Watts to the station in Milchester. They had now let him go, Julie understood.

'He wants to marry Mrs V.,' said Julie, 'like we all knew all along. But he knew Mrs V. wouldn't get any more money from Mr V. if she married again, not unless Mr V. was generous. He thought he could meet Mr V. and have a proper talk and explain everything, and that Mr V. would be a good loser and gentleman.'

'Fat chance.'

'Yes, but Ralph Watts had never met Mr V., and I suppose Mrs V. hadn't told him very much, and he thought he could appeal to Mr V.'s better nature. That's what I heard him saying to Dad. So he tried several times to meet Mr V., but Mr V. refused to talk to him. I suppose he knew Ralph Watts was after Mrs V., and he was jealous. So Ralph Watts had to trick him into a meeting.'

'Ah,' said Dan. 'Sophie away, Sylvia away, chance for Mr V. to grab the kid. That was the bait.'

'Yes, exactly. He knew it was chancy, but it was the only way he could think of to get face to face with Mr V. and appeal to his better nature.'

'Any proof of any of this?'

'Oh yes. He had letters Mr V. sent him, answering letters he wrote to Mr V. in Holland, refusing to meet him. Anyway he got word to Mr V. about Sophie being away and Anna being there, and he went off to meet him. That's why he left home on Saturday evening.'

'Clear so far.'

'But he got delayed. Road-works somewhere. He never did talk to Mr V. By the time he arrived at the Old Hall, it was buzzing with police and he panicked and ran away.'

'Anybody might. I did.'

'You did because you were in the house when Mr V. was shot. He did because he realized they could find out that he'd told Mr V. about Sophie being away. So they'd be bound to suspect him of the murder.'

'He had the motive, too.'

'Yes, he told Dad he'd thought of that.'

'You did some beautiful eavesdropping.'

Julie giggled. She said, 'When he was driving towards the house, he saw a man coming away. He just saw him for a moment, in his headlights. He didn't think anything about it, because he didn't know anything had happened. He didn't look closely at the man, or worry about it, until afterwards. Then he realized he'd probably seen the murderer.'

'Could he describe him?'

'A big fat man with a dark beard, wearing a sweater and jeans and a tweed cap.'

'Too much to hope he saw a boil on the bloke's neck.'

'Of course he didn't. I mean it's a pity, but of course he didn't.'

'What he says,' said Dan, 'all sounds true to me.'

'That's what Dad said. And the Super thought so too, according to Dad, because his description of the man matched Anna's.'

'So who told the big bloke that Piet Vandervelde was going to be there and Sophie wasn't going to be there?'

'They think it must have been somebody in Holland, in his office. They think he's probably made some terrible enemies in business, and his office would have known he was coming to England, to Medwell.'

'Likelier place for a leak, I do see that. Good thinking by the bluebottles. So now they're on to Interpol, and searching Amsterdam for boils?'

'I suppose so.'

'And searching for Ced . . . Anna?'

'Yes, of course, like mad, but Mrs V. isn't as worried as you might think. I mean, of course she must be worried out of her mind, but Anna keeps phoning, and she sounds perfectly happy, Mrs V. says, and she's in Warwickshire – she doesn't know where in Warwickshire, but she knows it's Warwickshire – and she's with some women. There hasn't been anything about a ransom, so they think it's frustrated old women who want children. Anna says she almost had breakfast in bed, according to Mrs V. Actually, Mrs V.'s more worried that they're spoiling Anna than mistreating her.'

'No reason anybody should be looking for me, then,' said Dan.

'Oh yes. They think you knew about the dog, and came to the Old Hall to burgle it, and burgled it, and then stole a lot of cars. Did you steal a lot of cars?'

'Borrowed a few . . . How do they think I knew about the dog?'

'They think you know everything. They think you spend all your time spying and prying and taking advantage.'

Dan reflected that this opinion, though harshly expressed, was not a bad sketch of his way of life.

He said, 'What do you mean, they think I burgled the Old Hall? Did somebody burgle it? Is anything missing?'

'Yes, some silver. They know you need money, to pay for your mother's operation. You didn't take more because you were interrupted. Oh, I've been to see your mother, to make sure she was all right.'

'That was kind. Was she?'

'Oh yes. She's cross with you, and she didn't want me to help her with the firewood and stuff, but I did. I'll go again tomorrow . . . All right, doctor, I expect to hear from you in the next day or two, thanks ever so much, bye-bye.'

Dan tried to make sense of all this, perched by the telephone in the beery back passage of the pub. He found it difficult. It went round and round in his head.

The first and most important thing was that Cedric's story was now proved to be true and her description of the murderer accurate. Little chilly notions had entered Dan's head that Cedric might have invented some or all of what she said she saw, in order to get Dan to take her away with him, in order to avoid punishment for midnight feasts and paint-sprays. These doubts were laid. Ralph Watts had seen the same man: there *was* such a man; and he was big and fat and dark and bearded, and he was the murderer. Cedric might lie to all sorts of people, but she had not lied to Dan. Dan felt ashamed of his half-formulated suspicions.

The next thing was that Ralph Watts's puzzling disappearance was now explained. His reappearance was easy to understand – he could not hide wherever he had been hiding for ever, and his story was credible and not really discreditable. He wouldn't want Sylvia to impoverish herself by marrying him; indeed, he probably knew Sylvia wouldn't marry him if it meant impoverishing herself. Sweet reasonableness with Piet Vandervelde would have been worth trying. Actually it wouldn't, but you had to know Piet to know that.

It was no longer possible to believe, as Dan had been prepared to believe, that Ralph Watts had hired the bearded man to kill Piet Vandervelde. No employer of a killer gives the police a description of his employee. There could be no connection whatever between Ralph Watts and the bearded man, and that must be as obvious to the police as it was to Dan, since the police had let Ralph Watts go.

The leakage of the news about Sophie and about Piet Vandervelde's plans was indeed more probable in Piet's Amsterdam office than in Medwell. Secretaries took messages, booked airline tickets, got Hertz cars. They gossiped in the Ladies. Dan remembered enough about offices, from his remote and hated years in the bank, to picture an enemy of Piet's getting hold of all the useful facts; someone cheated or betrayed, someone burning with hatred. The logic was good. It just didn't happen to be true that the murderer was some Dutchman Piet Vandervelde had cheated. He was a swimming-bath attendant in Madwick.

Hired, if not by Ralph Watts, then by whom?

The answer was sickeningly obvious.

Hired by Sylvia.

Sylvia in never-ending terror of Anna's abduction by Piet. In never-ending fear of Piet himself, the violent and jealous millionaire. Unable to remarry without instant poverty. Feeling, of course, undiminishing hatred of the man who had beaten her and virtually killed her grandfather . . .

Sylvia, with local contacts. However could Ralph Watts, at the other end of England in Kent, have recruited a killer handy to Medwell, deep in the West Country? Sylvia could have done it easily, getting names from the police files to which her various committees gave her access. One contact leading to another. A telephone call, arranging a 'chance' meeting. A sheaf of £50 notes torn in half, the other halves to be delivered when the job was done.

How had Sylvia known that Ralph Watts was luring Piet to the Old Hall? Because he had told her. He was her boyfriend, her lover, he wanted to marry her, and, as far as Dan knew, she wanted to marry him. He was trying to organize their financial future. Of course he had told her; she, equally obviously, had not told Ralph what she was planning – what bloody use she was making of his stratagem.

If Dan could do this unwelcome sum, so could the police.

The Detective Chief Superintendent – the one who looked like a fox – was a clever bastard, as Dan had cause to know. It must be a line that had occurred to them, as well as the attractive mirage in Holland.

Brooding, Dan realized that there was no coincidence anywhere at all. Everything followed, cause and effect. It was not even a coincidence that Dan himself had been, that same complicated night, in Julie's bed in that same house.

The only thing in the least like a coincidence was that Anna should have been downstairs having a midnight feast in the larder. And even that wasn't much of a coincidence: by her own account, she had midnight feasts pretty regularly.

A woman's voice had reported the murder before Julie had got around to reporting it. Who? Why? The answer must be Sylvia. Her hired gun had telephoned her in Kent the moment he was clear of the Old Hall, probably from the box outside the Medwell post office. She would have given him the Watts's number in Kent, and probably a phrase in code – say, 'Your car's fixed', meaning okay; something else meaning failure. She had then immediately rung the Milchester police. Why? To make things easier, less macabre, for Anna and Julie? It hardly would. So there might be an oddity in that telephone call, but it was the only oddity. Otherwise this explanation fitted all the known facts with a dreadful precision. Dan hated his new theory, but he was a long way towards believing it.

Was such a thing possibly true of Sylvia? Did she have a streak as tough as that? Dan remembered the Sylvia of their affair, clinging and giggling. He remembered that among her motives – prime among her motives – had been rebellion. She had giggled with excitement, and giggled at the thought of what her grandparents would say if they knew. In part, she had been using Dan as an instrument of rebellion; that was what their affair was about. When she clung, she was not being a frail clematis but a predatory boa-constrictor? Maybe that was a little hard. Dan found himself confused and unhappy contemplating Sylvia's psychology.

What did he want to do now? He and Cedric were about to catch and denounce the murderer. This would presumably get them both out of trouble, and was therefore still a good and necessary thing to do. But the murderer would, almost certainly, shop Sylvia. How about Cedric then? How about Sylvia?

Dan remembered his own words on the telephone to Julie: *'No reason anybody should be looking for me.'*

Julie had said yes, they were indeed looking for Dan because silver had disappeared and they thought he had taken it.

They might get to thinking a lot more than that. That Dan was . . .

What? An accomplice? An old friend of Sylvia's, once her lover, doing this job for her in collaboration with a big bearded brute from a swimming-bath? Why not? What would be improbable to the police about that? He wanted money and she had plenty, especially with Piet dead. You could reach the same point, even leaving Sylvia out of it. What was improbable about some resentful Dutchman hiring Dan to help, having learned from discreet local enquiry that he was the biggest villain unhung?

It was reaching a point where Julie was going to have to give Dan his alibi. Knowing Jim Gundry, that was a horrible thought. Anyway Julie might not be believed, since she had suppressed the truth about Dan's being there. Dan remembered the phrases from the sixth form at the grammar school: Julie would seem to be adding *suggestio falsi* to *suppressio veri*, and hiding the truth was as much of a lie as lying. Julie was in real trouble if she got Dan out of trouble.

Even if Julie were believed, Dan might still have nicked the silver on his way out. Dan supposed the murderer had nicked it, probably while waiting for Piet. It might even be part of his payment, Sylvia recouping from her insurance.

From a selfish point of view, the unmitigated disaster was Dan's bicycle.

'You look like a dying duck in a thunderstorm,' said Cedric. 'That's what we say at school.'

'Just how I feel,' said Dan. 'Complex bulletins. Outlook stormy.'

'What did Julie say?'

'Your mother's afraid you're being spoilt by the ladies that kidnapped you.'

'I am being spoilt,' said Cedric. She grinned suddenly at Dan. 'This is a lovely adventure.'

Dan grinned back, feeling oddly enriched.

He gave her a heavily expurgated account of Julie's electrifying news. He continued to conceal the identity of the corpse, and said nothing from which Cedric might deduce Dan's new theory about her mother.

Cedric seemed pleased, but not surprised, that Ralph Watts had cleared himself and gone home.

'I bet it was two burglars,' said Cedric positively. 'One shot the other because he was horning in on his territory – like bootleggers used to, all the time. Or Chinese pirates. Lieutenant Cedric Maltravers was always fighting Chinese pirates. The two burglars both knew Mummy and Sophie were away, because . . . because PC Gundry told them. He's a bent cop, like in a film I saw.'

'I don't think he is,' said Dan.

'You don't know him very well. Mummy does. She said, "Gundry's a rabbit". That was when he wouldn't arrest Mr Goldingham at the Chestnut Horse for staying open a bit late. Our gardener George Barrow said, "They rabbits ben a thieven plague". If PC Gundry is a rabbit, and rabbits are a thieven plague, it means PC Gundry is a thieven plague. That means he steals things. That means his friends are burglars. So there you are.'

Dan did not feel strong enough to challenge this remorseless logic. Anyway, it was a good thing for Cedric to believe, for as long as possible, that only rival burglars were involved.

There had been early frosts, bringing down great sodden drifts of leaves, and browning the edges of the petals of surviving flowers. Then the dying year had rallied, as though given a shot of monkey-gland; a St Martin's Summer had come a fortnight before Martinmas. Dan and Cedric had been very lucky, but their luck was ending.

Even while they were in the pub, the wind had changed and risen. It was gusting from the south-west, carrying clouds that grew blacker and blacker. Rain was imminent, slashing horizontal rain of the most unpleasant kind.

Cedric had no clothes for this sort of weather. Nor had Dan, but he was used to soakings; he was weathered by more than thirty years of autumn storms; he had not been pampered by a rich mother; he was not a little skinny girl of nine. He was worried about Cedric.

Cedric was not worried about herself. She said, 'If our clothes get wet and we can't dry them, we'll buy some more.'

Dan saw the force of this: they had plenty of money between them. But he was not used to so debonair an attitude. He thought he would never have a rich mentality, even if he became rich, which was as unlikely as his staying out of prison, unless they found the big fat man with the boil, whom both Anna and Ralph Watts had seen.

The rain came, even as they stood in the door of the pub. It was like being flayed with a wire cat-o'-nine-tails.

'Yow,' said Cedric, and shot back into the pub.

Dan followed her. It solved the immediate problem of how to keep dry for the moment: but not the problem of getting to Madwick, and all the other problems that attended and followed that.

A girl who was wiping down the bar said there was a bus to Madwick at three-thirty. Cedric made a face at the mention of a bus: it was not her way of travelling. But Dan felt an unusual reluctance to borrow any more cars. There were only two cars parked by the pub, and Dan had tried their doors, out of habit. Both were locked. The middle of the village in the middle of the day was no situation to be borrowing cars.

The rain lashed the windows of the pub, making efforts to smash the glass that seemed certain to succeed. Dan remembered the bus stop in the middle of Beeston, opposite the post office. It was very exposed, with a bench, but no shelter. Wildly Dan pictured getting under the bench while they waited for the bus.

Buses in these out of the way places were unpredictable. Dan imagined that the service from Beeston to Madwick was as capricious as that from Medwell to Milchester. The timetables were at best an approximation arrived at by an incurable optimist, at worst a practical joke designed to betray travellers into fruitless and interminable waiting.

That was all right in the summer.

Dan still didn't want to borrow a car, because to do so would have been crowding his luck indeed. He still didn't want Cedric to get soaked, with nothing dry to change into. He still did want to go to Madwick, to identify Piet Vandervelde's murderer.

'If we go swimming we'll be getting wet on purpose,' said Cedric. 'So it doesn't matter getting wet by mistake.'

'Question of raiment,' said Dan. 'Matter of garb.'

'We can wait for the bus in the telephone box.'

'Somebody may want to phone. Telephone.'

'They can't if we're using it. Wait a mo.'

She disappeared somewhere into the back of the pub. Dan supposed she was scrounging food, having finished lunch a full twenty minutes earlier. She reappeared with two immense raincoats, rubbery, dragging them because together they were too heavy for her to lift. Both coats were made for giants of prodigious height and girth. The idea of Dan wearing one was ludicrous; the idea of Cedric wearing one flatly impossible. The owner or owners of the coats might also take a view about their removal, and Dan was not anxious to tangle with a man or men of such size.

He shook his head at Cedric, attempting an expression of grave and considered judgement from which there could be no appeal. He had never tried making such a face before, and was a good deal surprised when it worked.

Mutinously Cedric let the monstrous garments fall. 'What, then?' she said.

'Rain's easing,' said Dan, hoping it was true. 'I suppose we could wait in the post office.'

'Do they sell Mars bars?'

'Every sort of bar you ever heard of,' said Dan recklessly, hoping this was also true.

It was a five-minute walk from the edge of the village to the post office in the middle. If the rain was easing, it was not easing much: they were both soaked before they were half-way there. No other pedestrians were about, and almost no cars. A few little cars were parked outside the cottages and council houses. Cedric tried the doors, still hoping for a more congenial mode of transport than the bus, but they were all locked. The rain was directly in their faces. Dan's banker's suit, rolled up in a bundle with his tie round it, was as saturated as the clothes he had on.

They reached the post office more wet than alive. Dan was surprised to find the cramped little shop thronged with children, a dense mass of noisy children of about Cedric's age, but not so wet because better equipped for the weather. The children were in the nominal charge of a man with a moustache who bleated at them. It was a school expedition, the whole of a form, or two forms, of the Beeston Primary School. All the children carried plastic or towelling bags. A picnic? In this weather? The plastic bag of one child was up-ended by a tiny bully. A towel and a swimsuit fell on to the floor of the post office, to be trampled by a score of sneakered or gumbooted feet.

The children were going swimming in the bath at Madwick.

'So be ye ben goen t'swimmen-pool?' said Cedric.

'You do talk common,' said a little girl. Dan restrained Cedric from attacking her.

The bus arrived, only twenty minutes late, jetting streams of spray from its wheels. The children surged out of the post office, screaming disapproval of the rain. Dan and Cedric surged with them. The teacher with the moustache bleated in the rear.

Dan saw a police car pull up just behind the bus, and a policeman in a uniform raincoat ran from the car to the post office.

Dan did not have to try to think quickly, his thoughts rushed at him unbidden. The fingerprints on the Renault which they had abandoned early that morning (it seemed a month ago), burglar, car thief, probable accomplice in a murder, biggest villain unhung. If caught now, unmasked also as kidnapper. Known to have come to Beeston with youthful companion, known to have been bound for Christie Wykes's. No doubt seen going into the post office to ask directions. Exact description to hand, including description of clothes now wearing. Description of youthful companion and 'his' clothes.

Dan dropped into a crouch and wriggled, knees bent, into the middle of the moving pack of children. They thought it was a joke but a bad joke. They thought Dan was being a stupid sort of funny uncle, sucking up to them by playing the fool, behaviour with which they were familiar from Halloween parties in the Women's Institute Hut, from Christmas parties in the War Memorial Hall. They said so. If the police car's windows had been open, the policemen in it alert and intelligent, and the road quiet, the pointed remarks of the children would have conveyed that, in their midst, an adult was trying to hide himself. But the car's windows were closed against the rain, and the rain thundered on the sides and roof of the bus and the car, and slapped into the puddles in the gutters and on the asphalt of the street. It saved Dan from discovery.

He and Cedric climbed on to the bus with the children. There was a moment when the business of getting on the bus obliged the pack of children to form a sort of single file. The door of the bus was a bottleneck. It was impossible for Dan to mount the step and go through the door behind the cover of the children. If he straightened he would be visibly an adult; and an adult up to that second deliberately hiding, known to the police, biggest villain unhung. If he continued his crouch he would be visibly a lunatic. He seized Cedric round the shoulders, and they squeezed through the door side by side. The children behind thought it was still a lousy joke, and said so. If the police car's windows had been open, Dan must have been exposed.

Cedric was very wet. She said she was fine, and was looking forward to swimming. Dan was looking forward to her identifying, with utter certainty, the man she had seen on Saturday night.

The bus went slowly, stopping often, and it had quite a long way to go. Dan had time to think, in spite of the nonstop deafening noise of the children round them. The other passengers on the bus were obliterated by the children. Dan was glad to think that he was obliterated, too; he could stop worrying for the moment and concentrate on thinking.

Cedric had seen Sylvia talking to the bearded man in the Stepleton Underhill antique shop. Of course she had not been asking about a set of chairs; of course she had not mistaken the man for the shopkeeper. They had made a rendezvous on the telephone, and were meeting 'casually' in that well chosen place, where it was feasible to browse indefinitely without attracting notice and easy to have a conversation without being overheard. This had been months before. Sylvia was then recruiting her employee and waiting for the moment. Since she had never mistaken him for an antique dealer, his accent and manner and class, which had so puzzled Dan, were no longer any kind of factor in the riddle. The whole antique shop was a red herring. The man was a yob; he rode a bicycle and he cadged lifts, like Dan himself. He had probably been working as a waiter or a porter in the brewer's marquee at the races. He was probably not a swimming instructor or a lifeguard at the baths, but the man who stoked the boiler for the central heating and the showers. He had no connection with Christie Wykes's yard: he was just a poor yob who had wanted a lift and invented a hard-luck story to get it. For the first time, the picture was consistent, and it fitted with a sawn-off shotgun.

Unfortunately, it was Sylvia who made the picture consistent. The antique shop episode, innocently reported by Cedric, now made everything fall into place.

High time too, thought Dan; but he wished very much it wasn't Sylvia.

9

Dan's clothes dried on him gradually, in the warmth of the bus. He was in only moderate discomfort when they arrived at Madwick.

Dan had never before been inside a public swimming-bath. Nor had Cedric: her school had its own pool, and in the summer there were various pools in people's gardens at which she and her mother were welcome.

'I haven't been swimming since the summer holidays,' said Cedric. 'I love swimming. I suppose I can borrow a costume, or hire one. I wonder what colour. I want a red one. I hope they heat the water.'

Dan hoped so too. He hoped Cedric would remember why they were there.

Dan was admitted to the building but not to the pool: not to the water or its immediate surroundings. It was a children's day, children under twelve only, supervised groups from local schools. There were several other groups, and the place swarmed with excited children. Cedric was absorbed into the crowd. From her point of view, it was fortunate that more than one school was represented. Everybody thought she came from somewhere else.

Dan was sent to a sort of public gallery far above the pool, with a few other depressed adults. He could not imagine what they made of him. It would have been better to have reverted to banker: but his banker's suit was still damply rolled up in a bundle. He looked like a poacher carrying something to go to the cleaner's, and did not fit at all with the shopkeepers' wives with whom he shared the public gallery. They thought so too. They fraternized with one another, but turned away from him with sniffs. In Dan's experience, the sniffs of shopkeepers' wives in the presence of their social inferiors were louder than all other sniffs, and the sniffs at the swimming-pool were the loudest he had ever heard. Of course, they too had been caught in the rain.

Dan saw that Cedric had somehow come by a swimsuit. He hoped she had hired or borrowed it from some official of the place, but he thought not. It was red. Dan saw her advance towards the girls' changing-room. A scandalized woman headed her off, a beefy female in a white flannel skirt as though she were about to play bowls. Cedric, headed towards the boys' changing-room, hung back. It was a problem she had not faced: one which had not occurred to Dan, either.

Cedric disappeared into the boys' changing-room, her cheeks as crimson as the borrowed swimsuit.

The pool was large and oblong, with a cluster of diving boards at one end. It smelled powerfully of chlorine, and looked astonishingly blue. Dan, whose swimming was done in rivers and for a purpose, realized that the blue was painted on the sides and bottom of the pool, and was not, as he had at first supposed, the colour of the water itself. He felt very country-mouse when he made this discovery. Nobody in whose garden he pretended to work, round Medwell Fratrorum, had a private pool. It was not a pool-owning village.

Over the impossibly blue pool arched a utilitarian structure of steel girders and concrete. There was a little natural light and a lot of artificial light. As a setting for fun, it was as joyless as a railway station in a manufacturing city, but the children shrieked and splashed under the eyes of adults in track suits.

None of the attendants visible had a beard. None was very big or fat. None had an evident boil on the neck, or a piece of sticking-plaster where a boil might be.

Cedric jumped in and climbed out and jumped in, dressed as a boy, in trunks. She looked like a skinny little boy. Probably she would continue to do so for another four or five years, after which this particular disguise would become impracticable. Evidently the water was warm enough, though it looked very cold from above in its false Arctic blueness.

A man who had a job at the pool, some kind of cleaner or

maintenance man, came fussily into the gallery. Dan asked him about a very big, fat man with or without a beard. The cleaner suspected a trap or an insult or a cruel joke, and Dan got nothing out of him. Dan was not allowed to go to the poolside to ask the people in track suits about a big fat man. In trying to do so he would have made himself the centre of unwelcome attention. He would have to leave it to Cedric. He tried to keep an eye on Cedric, in the noisy swarms of children.

Cedric's approach to bathing was long on enthusiasm but short on variation. She took a running jump at the water; while in the air, she folded her knees to her chest, clutched them, and smote the water rolled up into a ball. Her impact made a big splash. It was unpopular with children swimming nearby and with the guardian adults. When she surfaced, her cropped hair was glued to her skull. Her ears seemed to stick out more than ever. Had they flapped she could have flown. She swam a few strokes of breaststroke to the nearest ladder, climbed out, evaded censorious adults, and did exactly the same again. Again and again. Dan remembered jumping in in exactly the same way when he was small. You called it a 'honeypot' in those days. Water went up your nose, but otherwise it was very satisfactory. Probably Cedric's generation had a more sophisticated name for it.

Dan saw Cedric acquire a towel. He did not see how. The quickness of her hand deceived his eye. One moment she had no towel, the next she had a big pink towel enveloping her. Some other child would have no towel, or would have a wet towel. There was nothing Dan could do about that.

In her pink toga, Cedric was talking to one of the attendants, asking him about a big man who worked here, or had worked here. No doubt she mentioned beard and boil. Dan was pleased with her. She had not forgotten, even in the excitement of doing honeypots. At the very least she would get a name.

Dan thought Cedric was shivering. He thought she had been swimming long enough. He tried to communicate this view, telepathically, to the skinny little figure in the pink towel. But Cedric dropped the towel, and smashed into the water in another honeypot.

She had a green towel when Dan next saw her. She disappeared with it into the boys' changing-room. With the green towel, and with the name of the man who had shot her father.

'Terry Corbett,' said Cedric.

Her hair was still wet, but her clothes were pretty dry. She said she had put her knickers on a hot pipe in the boys' changing-room. They were eating fish and chips out of *The News of the World*, in a shop made entirely of formica near the baths. Swimming had given Cedric an appetite.

'Terry Corbett,' repeated Dan, bells of joy ringing about his head. 'Still working there?'

'No. He was sacked.'

'For murdering people?'

'I don't think so. I don't think they know about that. He was sacked for making an indecent assault.'

'Another of those. I don't want to hear about it.'

'I did, but they wouldn't tell me.'

'Did they tell you where he lives?'

'He did live at Stepleton Underhill.'

'That fits. That's why you saw him there twice. Eliminates coincidence. *Did* live at Stepleton?'

'Yes. He was turned out of his house.'

'More indecent assault?'

'I expect so. Yes, that was it. So he's got a new house and a new job.'

'Go on,' said Dan, trying to remember the words of prayers.

Cedric did not reply at once, since her mouth was full of fish and chips. It was a circumstance which did not always deter her from speaking. Dan thought it would not have done so now, but that her mouth was so full she was simply unable to speak.

Dan waited while Cedric chewed and swallowed. He had finished his own helping, a far smaller one than hers. Her face was pale under the strip-lighting. She might have been supposed peaky, overtired, undernourished. Tired she might have been after the exertions of the swimming-pool, but undernourished she certainly was not.

Three thoughts filled Dan's mind, as he watched the rhythmic working of Cedric's narrow little jaw. He was about to hear where the murderer was, and what he was now doing: that was good. If Cedric identified the murderer, and Dan and Cedric exposed the murderer, it seemed probable to the point of certainty that Sylvia would be revealed as the hirer of a bought gun; as accessory before, during, and after the fact of her husband's violent death: that was bad. And there would come a moment when Cedric herself would face the fact that the corpse she had seen, with a hole blown in its chest, was her own father: that was bad.

Cedric was spoiled, wilful, and deceitful. She was a brat. In her there was a lot of Sylvia's intolerable, intrinsic snobbery; there was a lot of Piet Vandervelde's ruthless arrogance. But there was a lot else too, and that other lot, in spite of the snobbery and the arrogance, or maybe in magic combination with them, made her one of the most completely congenial people Dan had ever known. You couldn't say she was good, exactly, but she was good company. Dad did not want her hurt.

Still she chewed. Her face was empty, impenetrable. She was thinking entirely about fish and chips. Chewing, she unscrewed the top of the ketchup bottle on the table, and dunked in it a long, soggy chip. She added the dollop of ketchup on the chip to the half-masticated mixture in her mouth. She glanced up, self-consciously, and saw the disapproval in Dan's eye. She giggled. She managed to giggle without spitting out any of the mush in her over-full mouth. She looked like a disgraceful, ill-mannered, delinquent little boy. She looked adorable.

Dan found his position, moral and emotional, extremely complex. Still, he had to know where to find Terry Corbett, and he had to wait for Cedric to finish her mouthful.

Cedric swallowed, and said, 'He doesn't live at Stepleton Underhill any more, but I don't know where he does live.'

'Oh,' said Dan.

'But I know where he works.'

'I hoped you did.'

'At a comprehensive school, in Madwick. Here. He stokes

the boilers or something. There's a man at my school who stokes the boilers, and *he'd* murder *anybody*.'

'You know what the school's called?' said Dan carelessly. 'You know where it is?'

'Yes, of course. It's called the North Hill School. I don't suppose it's on a hill at all, but it's called North Hill. Some boys at the swimming-pool go there. They were talking about it in the changing-room.'

Cedric blushed, at memories of the changing-room.

'Did they talk about Terry Corbett?'

'No, I don't think so. Why should they talk about the man who stokes the boilers? They were talking about Halloween. Did you know today is Halloween?'

'Gum, so it is,' said Dan. 'Thirty-first. Lost touch with dates, living like gipsies.'

He reflected that, some six hours later, it would be three days exactly since Piet Vandervelde was shot. It seemed three years, and also three minutes.

'The North Hill School gives a Halloween party,' said Cedric. 'That's what the boys were talking about. The whole school come to the party, in fancy-dress. It's a competition, with prizes. Somebody comes and judges. They did say who, but I've forgotten. Lovely prizes, given by the Rotor Club, or something.'

'Rotary,' suggested Dan. He had only the vaguest picture of the Rotary Club and its functions. He was not by nature a joiner of any club, least of all one composed of local business-men.

'They'll have to be warm,' said Cedric.

'The Rotary Club?'

'No, silly. Well, I s'pose *they'll* have to be warm too, but I meant all the children dressed up as – what do you think they'll be dressed up as?'

'Imagination boggles,' said Dan.

'Mine doesn't. Actually I don't know what 'boggles' means. What does it feel like to boggle? Would I know if I was boggling?'

'The children will have to be kept warm,' said Dan, 'so the

man who stokes the boiler will be there stoking away at the boiler.'

'That's what I thought. And I thought that if they're all going in fancy-dress, I could go too, in fancy-dress, and nobody would know I didn't belong to the school. I might win a prize. A car, or a yacht. Or a pony.'

'And in your disguise,' said Dan, 'you can prowl about and find the boilers, and show me the man who stokes them.'

'Yes, if you like. I don't know if they'll let you in.'

'I'll come as an uncle. What fancy-dress will you wear?'

'I don't know. The party doesn't start till seven, so we've got lots of time.'

'The shops are shut.'

'I wasn't thinking of *buying* anything.'

'Hum,' said Dan, wondering which of the two of them had a worse influence on the other.

The girl behind the counter of the fish-and-chip shop – a cheerful, meaty girl in a skimpy white overall, in whom, under different circumstances, Dan might have taken an interest – had herself been to the North Hill Comprehensive. She told Dan where it was. The Halloween party was a new tradition, inaugurated since her day. She thought it was silly, giving a lot of kids prizes for dressing up in their mothers' clothes. Her name was Debbie, which afforded Dan the minimum of surprise.

Cedric considered borrowing Debbie's overall, a policeman's uniform, or a jockey's boots, breeches and racing silks.

'You'll need a mask, if you're going to gatecrash,' said Dan.

The word 'gatecrash' was new to Cedric. She was pleased with the picture it presented, of the Incredible Hulk or of a heavy tank pulverizing obstacles of steel and concrete. She was pleased with the idea of a mask, too.

Cedric's section of *The News of the World* was at last totally denuded of fish, chips, vinegar, and ketchup. She looked at the greasy newspaper with a kind of nostalgia, as though it represented for her a distant, golden, unrepeatable experience.

She said, 'I must ring up Mummy again.'

'Why?' asked Dan. 'You talked to her this morning.'

'She'll start getting worried about me if I don't ring up.'

'She must be worried about you, even if you do.'

'I'll say I've just had a nice little tea. I won't say anything about the Halloween party. Mummy wouldn't want me to doorcrash.'

'Gatecrash.'

'Doorcrash is better. There might not even *be* a gate, but there's certain to be a *door*.'

Dan could think of no answer to this. He did not try. Debbie let Cedric use a telephone in a room behind the shop. Debbie thought Cedric a sharp little boy for his age.

Dan smoked the whole of two king-size cigarettes while Cedric telephoned.

She came back excited. 'I spoke to Uncle Ralph as well as Mummy. He's staying at home. At our home, I mean, not his home. The police want him where they can reach him. Mummy wants him where she can reach him, too. He's helping her to find me.'

'In Warwickshire?'

'He said he was giving her moral support. What's moral support?'

'What you and I give each other.'

'We give each other fish and chips. Mummy never lets me have fish and chips out of a newspaper. So Uncle Ralph's sister is coming to stay as well. To be a pineapple.'

'I doubt it.'

'Some sort of fruit.'

'A gooseberry,' suggested Dan. 'Third party. Protects reputation. Why gooseberry I don't know.'

'And I don't know what you're talking about,' said Cedric. 'We must go and find my fancy-dress.'

Sylvia was losing no time, thought Dan. Her husband had been dead about sixty-five hours, and she already had her boyfriend in the house. With a gooseberry. Moral support: it looked all right but it wasn't, not if you knew how her husband had died.

123

Terry Corbett, three streets away, stoking the boilers in a Comprehensive.

It couldn't have been indecent assault that got him sacked from the swimming-bath; at least it seemed unlikely to Dan that he would have been re-employed, immediately, in a school. Straight assault, without the indecency, seemed more likely. It was still odd that a school took him on, unless he had influential friends.

He had Sylvia. She was influential, all over the county. She probably had nothing directly to do with a school twenty-five miles from her own village, but she almost certainly knew some of the school governors, and people in the County Education Authority, if that was what it was called. Dan knew nothing about the tentacles of power within the Establishment, but he imagined that a few telephone calls in the right quarters could get anybody any job. Probably the guarantee of a job was part of the fee Sylvia was paying Terry Corbett. Dan was shocked, contemplating privilege and corruption in high places. Jobs for the boys, even if they were hired murderers with boils on their necks.

Two drab-coloured buses, in line ahead like elephants, stopped at traffic lights outside the fish-and-chip shop.

'Soldiers,' said Cedric with scorn.

Both buses were indeed full of very young soldiers in battle-dress, their hair clipped as close as Cedric's. Dan thought they were boy soldiers, and his heart went out to them in pity. Being shouted at, being punctual, doing everything by the book, conforming absolutely – he would have died of their life. Those boys were all volunteers; they had chosen to submit to discipline, to doing everything in a group, to doing exactly what everybody else was doing. That was the most pitiable aspect of it. It was as though Dan had chosen to stay in the bank: lunacy; purgatory.

Impatient to equip herself with fancy dress, though not yet clear how this was to be done, Cedric bounced restlessly round the fish-and-chip shop. She went to the window to look at the scrubbed young soldiers in the buses. She compared them unfavourably with sailors and – glancing at Dan, quite kindly –

even with Marines. She watched the buses start when the lights changed, rumble forward for fifty yards and then stop again. They stopped outside the swimming-bath. Fifty youths in battledress trickled off the buses. They carried rolled-up towels. It was to be assumed that, like the schoolchildren, they had swimming trunks inside their towels. There were older men with them, a sergeant-major and some sergeants and corporals. The sergeant-major did not fall his party in, but shoo'd them informally into the grey building which housed the bath.

'Rabble,' said Cedric.

They straggled in, looking fairly cheerful about swimming. Dan deduced that being taught to swim was part of their training nowadays. He supposed it was a good idea, dimly imagining amphibian operations in which thousands of boy soldiers swam ashore in regimental swimming-trunks.

Cedric thought it was a very good thing. She wanted to go and watch the soldiers being taught to dog-paddle. Dan demurred; he had had enough of those depressing, chlorine-reeking vaults. He wanted another cup of coffee. He wanted to chat up the cheerful Debbie. He decided also to change his clothes, to improve their chances of doorcrashing the Halloween party. Cedric could come to no harm, amid all those alert corporals. She could do harm, but hardly suffer it. Dan told her to be back in twenty minutes.

Dan changed in the back room, and invited Debbie to help him change. He thought she would have done so, but customers came in.

Dan's banker's suit was damp and wrinkled. It seemed to steam when he put it on in the warmth of the fish-and-chip shop. He tied his tie carefully, but he was definitely not a Captain of Marines. He was a bank-clerk who had been caught in the rain. His tie, which all day had secured the bundle of his clothes, was like a wet bootlace.

Debbie gave a little scream when he emerged and asked her for more coffee. She had expected a sly hobbledehoy, not a damp bank-clerk. Dan winked at her.

Cedric reappeared in much less than twenty minutes. She

hurried in carrying a large bundle imperfectly wrapped in newspaper.

'My costume,' she said, with an expression of suspicious innocence. 'I got it at the Oxfam shop for 75 pence. There's the Oxfam shop.'

There indeed it was, on the other side of the street. It looked shut, but Cedric said she had just got there in time.

'Want to change here, sonny?' said Debbie.

'I'll wait till we get there,' said Cedric.

She would not show Dan her costume. She said she wanted it to be a surprise. Dan wondered what grotesque finery Cedric had bought for 75 pence.

Dan whispered a promise to come and see Debbie again. She was pleased. He slipped behind the counter and kissed her quickly and lecherously, in the cover of the coffee-machine. Following Debbie's directions, they walked the few hundred yards to the school.

The school was brilliantly lit. A lot of cars were parked in the big forecourt, under floodlights. Every window – big, healthful, modern windows – blazed with uncurtained lights. It was a very new building, mostly one-storey, made apparently of blue and white plastic. There were already a lot of people inside and more were constantly arriving – children and adults, groups of other children, on foot and on bicycles, noisy, in blackface or Red Indian headdresses or nurses' uniforms. Some were punks and some red-nosed clowns; they shrieked when they penetrated one another's disguises; they all knew each other, of course.

'You should have a mask,' said Dan.

'I'll see you later,' said Cedric.

Before he could stop her, Cedric disappeared with her bundle. Obviously her idea was to change somewhere out of sight, then infiltrate the party from behind. Really it was a good idea, saving her from the gauntlet of teachers on the way in. The cheerful, well-lit school was another place where she could do, but not come to, harm.

Dan decided on his own role as he approached the door in the wake of a scrum of small Wurzel Gummidges. He was glad he had thought of changing. His wrinkled suit and wet-boot-lace tie were no disadvantage in the role he chose.

A man who had the air of being in charge looked at him enquiringly.

'Ralph Maltravers, *Milchester Argus*,' said Dan, in the qualified bank-manager voice he thought right for a local reporter. 'Not really here officially. Haven't even got my press card. Just heard of this beano and thought you wouldn't mind my looking. Might be a piece in it for my paper. Editor approves of this sort of shindig. Of course we're outside your area, but blood's thicker than water, eh?'

The utter meaninglessness of this last phrase, which popped out before Dan could censor it, seemed not to bother the head teacher.

'You're very welcome, very welcome,' Dan was told, as he expected. He was glad he had not represented himself as the Commandant of the local Army Cadets, the Chairman of the Rotary Club, or a detective inspector of police, all of which had occurred to him.

He sauntered benignly among shrieks, drenched with music from a crackling public-address system. He was looking for Cedric and for Terry Corbett.

'Us d'jus' shift hereabouts,' said a childish voice with a very broad country accent. ''At's why ye dun knows we, a-do b'lieves.'

The speaker was the centre of a group of children, more or less unimaginatively costumed. He was a small, skinny boy in garments meant for a large man. His trousers bagged like a malfunctioning hot-air balloon, and completely hid his feet. His sleeves were twice as long as his arms. His hat covered most of his face. He was in uniform. He was dressed as an army sergeant, three bold chevrons on each sleeve, medal-ribbons on the left breast, a dark-blue beret with a shiny brass regimental badge.

Oxfam shop? Cedric had revisited the changing-room at the swimming-bath.

Meanwhile she had equipped herself with a tray of sausage rolls, which she was sharing, reluctantly, with her new friends.

The classrooms of the school were bright with maps and pictures and childish paintings. One class had been making mobiles, cardboard cutouts on nylon thread, which revolved slowly. It was all very warm. The central heating was effective, even excessive. Boilers, thoroughly stoked.

Dan came by a notebook and a pencil, carelessly left by somebody in a desk. He took notes, not ostentatiously, but careful to be seen doing so. A conscientious reporter to his fingertips, he strolled away from the hubbub and the public places into echoing back premises where things were stored. He found large, ultramodern kitchens, where mothers and teenage girls were assisting the staff.

He found a place of lagged water-tanks, coiling pipes, and electronic controls.

He looked blankly at the boilers, not at first realising that boilers were what he was looking at. There were four neat white metal boxes with transparent panels in front, and thermostats and switches above. He peered into one. A gas pilot-light glowed blue. There was a sudden whoosh, and a sheet of disciplined orange flame. The thermostat had turned on the gas.

Nobody stoked boilers of this sort: they were completely automatic. Somebody gave them a quick brush-out twice a year. Such boilers were not known in the Medwell area, which was far from the nearest gas-main, but Dan had seen them in modern buildings in Milchester.

Whatever Terry Corbett did, he did not stoke boilers.

Dan goggled at the boilers, completely puzzled.

A memory came to him, unbidden, completely inexplicable except as the result of a mysterious but fruitful subconscious process. He remembered Cedric in the pool – a skinny little white body in boy's swimming trunks, white chest, legs, arms. A white left forearm. No purple dye, or so little it was invisible at a distance.

And all at once Dan understood.

He understood all about Terry Corbett, the big bearded man with the boil. He understood who had murdered Piet Vander-velde, and how and why.

He had been morally certain before, of one theory and then another and then a third. Now certainty transcended the moral and became rock-hard, copper-bottomed. He knew. There was no longer any room for doubt.

He was so astonished that he sat down suddenly, on the floor.

10

Very well, he had the knowledge. What was he going to do with it? Nobody else would believe a word of it.

He thought about the people involved, and where they all stood. He thought about Cedric, and how this would hit her. He thought about himself, and where he stood, and how it would hit him. The bicycle. The missing silver. His disappearance. Was he an accomplice? An accessory?

The police were looking for a man answering to Terry Corbett's description. They might by now have that name, which might or might not be a real one. Presumably they would go on looking till they found him. Other charges – against Dan, for example – would presumably wait. What did the police really think about the big bearded man with the boil? What did they think about his motive? Private grudge, interrupted burglary, a hired gun? But hired by whom? Had they done the sum as Dan had done it, and come out with Sylvia's name? How could they fail to add it up that way?

Dan seemed to himself to have a number of options, all more or less odious. He could do nothing, stay hidden (with or without Cedric) and let the police go on looking for Terry Corbett. He could reappear (with or without Cedric), with the best answers he could think of ready for the questions they'd ask him.

The first course had certain attractions, especially since Julie was looking after his mother as much as she was allowed to. Obviously it was not a long-term answer: life had to go on, his own as well as Cedric's, and Julie could not forever bring in his mother's firewood, and feed the dogs and birds. Besides, his continued disappearance could do his reputation no good.

And if he knocked on the door of a police station? 'Excuse

me, my name is Mallett. I've been away on a bit of a holiday. I'd like my bicycle back, if it's quite convenient . . .'

Julie and her Dad. That missing silver. Biggest villain unhung.

The third option was for him to prove the truth so that even the bluebottles believed it. It meant baiting a hook for the murderer, just as the murderer had baited a hook for Piet Vandervelde.

Dan thought about the bait, and his mouth was dry with fright.

He found himself on his feet again, going back into the shrieking party. He saw that VIPs had arrived – stout men in green suits, women with hair like silver barbed-wire. The children were slowly being pushed into groups, for the judging of the fancy-dress. Cedric, barely visible in her enormous beret, was being pushed into no group because she belonged with no group. There was a danger of her becoming isolated, forlorn, perhaps conspicuous.

There was no doubt that her fancy-dress was admired and envied – Dan had heard her offered 10p for it, then 15p. She was not open to offers, but an auction might develop.

A pink and comely girl was visible at the edge of the crowd. She wore a plastic raincoat over a white overall, and seemed to be searching about, urgent, anxious. It was Debbie. She saw Dan, and waved. With difficulty they met, keeping their heads above the waves of children who frothed about them.

Debbie tried to whisper to Dan, but it was necessary to shout.

She shouted, 'Sergeant lost his clothes. Your kid was seen comin' out of the room, and seen comin' into the shop. Two of them came and asked me where he went. I said here, I'm ever so sorry. When they asked, I didn't know about the clothes. Sergeant's borrowin' a pair of trousers, and on his way. I never saw a man so mad.'

Dan felt a surge of gratitude to this good-hearted girl. He found her hand and squeezed it. She grinned, as though rewarded.

Dan fought his way, pretending to take notes, through children who were now in groups for the judging, or were joining groups, or leaving groups they had joined. So far from being isolated, Cedric had become the nucleus of an unofficial group which resisted the efforts of teachers to disperse it.

She was raising her voice against the hubbub, but retaining her ludicrous accent. She had resumed the role, popular with the police, of abandoned child. 'Me Mam run off wi' a sojer,' she cried to her audience. 'Lef' 'is closis beyind, a-did, acos they run off in middle o' the night. Run off nekkid, a-did, acos me Dad foun' they a-rompen. Thicky yere ben 'is closis.'

Dan gestured to her from the edge of the group, commanding, imploring. She pretended not to see him. She was enjoying the doorcrashed party. With his chin on his shoulder, expecting any second the irruption of the enraged sergeant, Dan began to call to her, softly and then loudly. She pretended not to hear.

In desperation he reached out and grabbed one sticking-out earlobe. Cedric screamed. Dan pulled her mercilessly clear of her audience. She fought and whimpered.

Dan got it through to her that the sergeant was arriving, with a whip, and Cedric got out of the immense uniform quicker than Dan would have believed possible. She simply wriggled, and the billowing garments were in a heap at her feet. She'd been wearing her own clothes underneath.

A heavy-set, brick-faced man in improvised garments came into the school like a storm.

'I won't win without my costume,' said Cedric.

'No,' agreed Dan. 'Might as well go.'

Local reporter and doorcrasher made for the back way which the latter had previously established. The brick-faced man had already spotted his uniform on the floor, and was beginning to roar.

Dan said nothing to Cedric about the staggering discovery he had made twenty minutes earlier. It would all have to come out, but not yet. The worm is not instructed in his function, but simply skewered on the hook for the fish to gobble. Dan wondered if he had a landing-net strong enough for the fish he was after.

The fish-and-chip shop was now crowded with its early-evening trade, and Debbie had been joined behind the counter by a middle-aged man. It was no longer possible for Dan to thank her properly, or say good-bye to her properly, or use the telephone.

Cedric said it was time they had the use of a car again, and Dan agreed. They took one from outside the school.

The sausage-rolls she had eaten at the party had given Cedric an appetite. She was not allowed into the pub they stopped at, but Dan brought cheese sandwiches and pickles out to her. He telephoned Julie, who told him his mother was angry but otherwise all right. Julie had taken the lurcher and the terrier for a walk, but the pointer had refused to come.

Dan said, 'Have you got a friend you completely trust?'

'You,' suggested Julie, surprised.

'Besides me.'

'Man or woman?'

'Woman. Oh yes, woman. Any woman.'

'Round here?'

'No. Best a long way off. Like another girl from your college.'

Julie said there were three girls she completely trusted, one in Scotland and one in London and one somewhere in the East Midlands. She had their telephone numbers. She did not know if any of them would be at home.

Dan gave her instructions which worried and puzzled her.

He told her to make sure that the friend – whichever completely trustworthy friend she contacted – rang her back as soon as the friend had done what Julie asked her to do. Julie was then to ring Dan: he gave her the number of the coin-box in the pub. He told her to ask for Mr Maltravers, being for the moment unable to think of any other name.

He swore Julie to secrecy, and tried to reassure her. He told her to trust him. He thought she wanted to do so and was trying to do so, but she was still puzzled and alarmed.

Dan was alarmed, too.

Julie's call was a long time coming, three-quarters of an hour. Dan spent most of the time hanging about near the telephone. When the publican and his regulars looked at him oddly, he said he was waiting for news of his auntie, who was having an operation in Yeoville. Cedric got bored sitting in the car. It took another heavy meal to pacify her.

Julie rang. Dan took the telephone from the publican. The three friends Julie had tried had all been unavailable. A fourth friend, Irish but living in Liverpool, had done what Julie asked and had just rung to say so.

Dan thanked Julie passionately.

'Auntie will pull through,' he told the men in the pub. He made himself look far more cheerful than he felt.

The murderer had already given evidence of ingenuity and audacity. And of prodigious luck. The mechanics of the baited trap had to take account of all three – especially, maybe, the luck.

The idea was to dictate to the murderer, unknown to the murderer, not only where and when to come but also how. On foot. From a particular direction, on a particular route. The idea was, by this means, to oblige the murderer to declare, effectively, 'I did it'. And also to prevent the murderer's escape. And also to prevent another murder.

Dan thought he had a strong hand, though by no means an unbeatable one. The murderer would be expecting to see Anna, not Cedric – a child of the past, a long-haired and dainty little girl who no longer existed. The murderer would be expecting to see a woman, maybe in a red wig, not a poacher nor yet a still-almost-natty bank-clerk.

Maps had unrolled in Dan's mind – large-scale maps, not of these remote places where he and Cedric had played hide-and-seek with Terry Corbett, but of Dan's own back-yard, the vicinity of Medwell Fratrorum, where he knew every thorn-bush, bramble, tree-root and creepway. Where he knew every twist of the river, every marshy water-meadow, sedge-covered island, rickety fisherman's footbridge.

Cedric was sleepy after grossly over-eating unsuitable food. There was no rug in the new car. Dan changed out of his banker's clothes into his ordinary clothes, shiveringly, in the

Gents at the pub. He wrapped Cedric in the banker's coat, in the back of the car.

Just before the pub shut, Dan bought Pepsi-Cola and sausage rolls, it having been established that this was Cedric's preferred breakfast. He forgot the effect of his changed appearance on people, until he saw the effect. He and his companion would, unfortunately, be vividly remembered.

Dan drove his new car towards Medwell, feeling a sort of joy at increasingly remembered landmarks, in the headlights, which made him understand the emotions of Ulysses. Ulysses's dog, Dan thought, had given the returning warrior a passionate greeting. His own dogs would do the same. The thought was cheering. But it was not yet time to go home to Nimrod and the others. Much had to be done first.

Dan avoided the village itself. He struck the Milchester road from Medwell near Yewstop Farm. At the farm he turned off. He bumped along Willie Martin's farm road and on past the farm. He wanted to go nowhere near the buildings: Willie Martin had a pig of a dog. Beyond the farm, the made road became a deep-rutted track. Dan drove along it as quietly as possible. He did not need lights. He had come this way, times without number, in the dark: Willie Martin's riverwoods were a wonderful place for woodcock.

This was because the boggy woods gave the ground-roosting birds deep, almost impenetrable cover: and because on the other side of the loops of slow river there was an extensive, undrainable tract of marsh – woodcock feeding-ground. They stuck their long beaks into the mud, in the middle of the night, and pulled out the creepy-crawlies they liked eating. There was no mystery about that. The mystery was how they detected worms three inches deep in mud.

Slow rivers meander. Fast ones eventually cut a straight path through their valleys, as power of water scours away obstacles. Here below Medwell, this river wandered through marsh and water-meadow in extravagant loops. Here and there, floodwater or vain attempts at drainage had joined loops at their necks, the river taking an unhurried short cut. Thus islands had been formed, squashy and sedgy, useful only to wild birds.

This piece of river should have been useful to fishermen. The syndicate that had the trout-fishing hereabouts – Dr Smith, Admiral Jenkyn and the others – had tried to make this stretch fishable. They had spent a lot of money on the banks and on footbridges, for without bridges to the bits that had become islands, hundreds of yards of the river were unfishable. There was simply no way of getting to the water. Even if you went miles round, you had to splosh through acres of bog. The syndicate had built a fishing-hut, too, on an island in one of the loops of the river. This was because there was no cover nearby – nothing nearer than Willie Martin's river-woods – and the elderly members of the syndicate disliked being caught in the rain.

But it had all turned out too difficult and too expensive. The river changed character when it entered this marshy stretch: just above and below the village it was brisk and clear, and ran over sharp gravel, but here the bottom was all mud, the surface all flannel-weed, and it could not be turned into trout-fishing. One day one of the foot-bridges had collapsed under Admiral Jenkyn, who had suffered a wetting and a lacerated elbow; this had turned him and the other rods against the whole reclamation project. They abandoned this stretch of the river to pike and woodcock, sedges and waterhens. They abandoned it to Dan, who caught a lot of their stew-fed rainbow-trout, wandering down-river from the village, on worms and little shiny spoons: catching them out of season when rainbows, coming from the other side of the world, are actually at their best. Thus Dan knew the whole wet wilderness better than anybody else.

The collapsed footbridge had never been rebuilt. The others were intact but perilous. The fishing-hut still stood, but the roof leaked, the single window was broken, and the door had come off its hinges.

Nobody unfamiliar with these acres of tranquil decay would – or conceivably could – cross them at night. Therefore if Dan was in position, with his hook baited, before dawn, he would be safe from surprise.

Dan drove the car through the remembered ruts into Willie Martin's woods. The bottom scraped on the middle of the track between the ruts, and Dan mentally apologized to the owner. The track dwindled, so that it was something between a footpath and a stream bed. Dan pulled off it, into what he thought was fair cover. Cover for the car was not terribly important in the short term, for even if it were immediately identified, nobody could immediately trace it to Dan. He had not declared his intention of borrowing it from in front of the school, and had not been seen doing so. The tracing would come in time, of course. But by then one or more bombs would have gone up. There would either be no need to worry about anything minor, or it would be too late to worry about anything at all. Either way, a borrowed car more or less would be no more than an embarrassment.

When the car could plough no further into the undergrowth, Dan switched off and got out. He opened the back door with difficulty, against a wall of brambles and hazels. He stowed their breakfast into the poacher's pocket of his old tweed coat, in which there was room for a dozen breakfasts. The cans of Pepsi clinked. Dan picked up Cedric, still swaddled in the other coat, the banker's coat, and mumbling in her sleep. She was very light.

He wondered what to do with the key of the borrowed car, and concluded that it made absolutely no difference.

Dan's eyes were well accustomed to the clear darkness outside the wood, but under the soggy old trees even he had great difficulty picking his way. He did not want Cedric's eye poked out by a bramble. They made slow time through the undergrowth, until Dan found himself in one of the broad rides cut by the people who had the woodcock shooting. The rides had been useful to Dan when netting woodcock in the dawn in late summer; they were useful now. He stepped out towards the river. Cedric mumbling and Pepsi cans clinking.

It was now, Dan thought, exactly seventy-two hours since a hole had been blown in Piet Vandervelde's chest. He contemplated those seventy-two hours, feeling like a man overlooking some landscape of nightmare, some panorama of the impossible. The liberties taken by himself, in the way of borrowing property and identity, were comparatively normal and innocuous, not far removed from what was called for in the ordinary way of daily business: though it was true that he had never before crowded so many indiscretions into so short a time. He had also never before been a Captain of Marines. But at the outrages perpetrated by Cedric – several a day, even several an hour – the mind boggled.

Cedric had said she didn't know what boggling felt like. Her head was awkwardly pillowed on his right shoulder. Dan realized that he would be overjoyed to be at home, and thankful to be out of all this, and miserable to be out of all this.

He came out on to the riverbank. It had been cleared with axes and billhooks and then an Allen scythe; but Nature, pitchforked out, had returned. Briefly it had been possible, if not very profitable, to cast a dry-fly here; Dan had himself, from hiding, watched Admiral Jenkyn doing so, the day the footbridge had collapsed. Now it was impossible even for the Admiral, so deep a margin of sedges separated bank from water, so furiously had brambles and nettles and alder and hazel reinvaded their territory.

Dan could see better, but he had to go even more warily, because it was hard to tell where dry land ended and river began. Even by daylight here, you could plant a confident foot on a piece of firm green ground and suddenly be in eight feet of stinking water.

It did stink, not with sewage or carrion but simply with dead sedge, water-weed, wood, leaves, fungus. Some poet, dimly coming back to Dan from his days at the Grammar School, had rhymed 'rotten' with 'unforgettable, unforgotten' in describing the smell of a river. He had had it right.

Awkwardly if not onerously burdened by Cedric, Dan picked his way along the river bank. He was going at this moment more or less towards Medwell, which should have been upstream, but so crazily did the river loop in the marshes that he was going downstream. He knew exactly where he was. He looked for and found the footbridge that had given the Admiral his bath and his gash. You could see that there had been a bridge, but even in the dark you could see that there was one no longer. Only a bird could now cross that way to the island where the hut was – a dabchick, a water-vole, an otter. Of course, any-body who could swim could swim to the island, but why would anybody swim when there was another footbridge, near enough complete, two hundred yards further downstream, joining this bank (after a further wide loop) to the far end of the island?

Dan had thus dictated the murderer's route to the island.

He could see the island on his left, across a dozen yards of barely-moving, perfectly smooth, viscous water. There was very little current and no wind. The oily mirror of the water reflected the dome of the sky, starless and moonless but slightly paler than the black land, the tangled mass of the river-woods to Dan's right. The island showed as a shadow on a shadow, three hundred yards long and pear-shaped; a soggy and useless jungle, visited now, as far as Dan knew, by no courting couples, no poachers except himself, no anglers or wildfowlers: nobody. The hut was at the far end, the fatter end of the pear, the downstream end. The surviving footbridge was that end. It was not a proper footbridge, as the other had been; it was more durable but less comfortable, simply a log with a heavy wire at one side, a yard above it, stretched between posts, as a hand-rail. Chicken-wire had been tacked on the top of the log, to make a better surface for the fishermen's feet. It was perfectly all right for an active man, unburdened, in daylight. It was all right for Dan, carrying Cedric, in the dark, because he knew every inch of it. He knew where there were knots in the wood, and where the wire was frayed. Of course any active person, anybody with a lot at stake, could have crossed it in the dark, though they had never seen it before. But it had first to be found. It was difficult to spot, even at noon, the near end being hidden by billows of jungle which forced you away from the bank. Of course Harry Bassett, the water-keeper, would have found it in the dark, and probably Dr Smith also. Probably not the Admiral, or any other member of the fishing syndicate. None of those people were involved in this. Dan was as certain as he could be that the murderer would neither cross nor even find the footbridge before dawn.

By daylight you could find it if you had been told what to look for; and you would certainly cross it if that saved you from being convicted of murder.

Dan shifted Cedric as gently as he could, so that she hung over his left shoulder like somebody's greatcoat. This freed his right hand for the wire. It was too much to expect that she would sleep through this.

She squeaked, not knowing where she was or why she was being treated like a sack of potatoes.

'Still me,' said Dan softly.

'I know,' she said gummily. 'Now that I'm awake I'd rather walk.'

'Not this bit,' said Dan. 'You need to know where to put your feet.' He picked his way to the end of the footbridge.

'Hold still,' he said, as she wriggled.

'I'm scratching an itch.'

He had to let her scratch. It took a long time. He made her promise not to scratch any more, however bad an itch she had, until they were safely on the island.

He embarked on the footbridge, going very slowly, holding tight to the heavy wire handrail to his right. The river showed below, inches under the log, silent. There was a smell of decay from the bank behind and from the bank ahead.

Cedric whimpered. Dan stopped, surprised. It was not like her to be frightened.

She said, 'I've got to scratch again.'

Dan held tight to the wire, and gripped Cedric tight with his left arm, as the effort of scratching made her wriggle like a clockwork snake. He proceeded at last, slowly, slowly, putting one foot exactly in front of the other, feeling with his toes for irregularities in the log which by day would have been visible and harmless, thankful for the chicken-wire on the log and for the reassuring cable at waist height. The crossing would not have given him a moment of pause if he had been unburdened, or carrying an inanimate load. Concern for Cedric made him slow and tentative and nervous, although he knew objectively that the more confidently he went the safer he was.

He gave a large sigh of relief when he squelched into the mud of the island.

'Now I'll walk,' said Cedric. 'Where are we? Why are we here? What smells so peculiar? Is that a house? Are we spending the night here? What's for breakfast?'

Dan put her down. He answered all her questions except 'Why?'

They went to the half-ruined hut, twenty yards down the bank of the island from the footbridge. Inside there was a clammy atmosphere and a sense of millions of woodlice in the rotting planks. There was a kind of bench. Dan recommended it, but Cedric said it was too hard to lie on, or even to sit on. The banker's coat could be a mattress, but, if so, not an eiderdown. If an eiderdown, not a mattress. Dan took off his other coat, his old tweed coat. The cans clanked in the poacher's pocket. Dan unpacked them, and the sausage rolls in their greasy paper bag, and stowed them under the bench. The sausage rolls seemed to have welded themselves together, in the passage of woods and footbridge, into a single doughy lump. Dan gave Cedric the tweed coat as a mattress, and wrapped the banker's coat round her as an eiderdown. She thus lay softer: the other way round, she might have been warmer but her bed would have been harder. She fell asleep at once. Her period of extreme wakefulness had been a hiccup, or punctuation.

She could come to no harm, on a deserted island nobody could reach. Not until dawn. Her breathing was just audible. Dan could hardly see her, used as his eyes were to the darkness, inside the hut. There were no snakes or wolves or scorpions. Woodlice could run all over her sleeping face – probably would – without harming her. They might make her want to scratch another itch.

Cedric was as safe in the ramshackle fishing hut as she had been in Medwell Old Hall. Safer; there was no longer a father to come and get her. Safe, until dawn.

Very near the hut, under a drift of brambles, Dan poked for and found a plastic bag which had contained fertilizer. He prodded with confidence, and heard at once the rustle of the thick plastic. There had never been the slightest chance that anybody would ever look for, let alone find, this one of his many cached devices.

141

In the bag were some spools of heavy nylon monofilament fishing line, and hooks and spoons and a landing-net and other gear. All this was for the stock, stew-bred rainbow trout put into the river further up by Dr Smith and the fishing syndicate: trout at their natural best – whatever the game-laws said – in December and January. They came from south of the Equator, from Chile and the rivers of the Andes. Their clocks and calendars had not been changed like those of a jet traveller. Dan fished for them out of season without compunction.

The blue plastic fertilizer bag contained all his fishing-tackle for this place. For this reason he kept it here: it was easier and safer to keep things on the spot (as with the keys of borrowable cars) than to have things in his pockets when he was travelling. People who searched you and found nylon and hooks and spoons got not so much the wrong idea as – much worse – the right one.

Dan selected, by sure touch, a spool of 10-pound test line. It was absurdly heavy stuff for two-pound rainbows, in the ordinary way of sport: but not if you were fishing without a rod – without the elegant luxury of playing the fish against the whippy resilience of split cane. The nylon seemed absurdly light for what he wanted of it – the capture of an adult human being. But if you tried to break this stuff between your hands, you couldn't.

In thick undergrowth, in early dawn, it would be invisible.

Dan cut off ten lengths of the powerful, invisible nylon, ten-foot and eight-foot and six-foot lengths. He went to the island end of the footbridge. There was a kind of path between the footbridge and the hut, not a good path, but visibly the best way to go. By daylight, the dimmest of daylight, anybody going from the footbridge to the hut would go that way. Really it was the only way. Dan snared the path, ten times. In each length of nylon he tied a big loop, with a slip-knot. Using much finer nylon, he had done this in the dark a thousand times, laying his 'angles' for the pheasants. It was easier with this heavier stuff. He opened out the loops till they were a yard or more across, the full width of the path. He laid the loops close to the ground, on the almost-footpath. He laid a series of loops, almost overlapping, from the end of the footbridge on the way to the hut. He tied each end of each snare to something either side of the path – young willow, alder or hazel, growths themselves whippy, not readily breakable, their roots tenacious in the gluey soil.

This was deeply familiar work to Dan, but he took a long time over it because it had to catch and not let go.

At last all ten snares were in position covering the first half of the twenty yards between footbridge and hut. Dan sank back on his heels in the mud, and considered how things stood.

The murderer would come, because of the message from Julie's friend in Liverpool. At dawn, because it was impossible to come earlier. By the footbridge, because there was no other way to come. Along the path, because there was no other way from footbridge to hut. Into the snares.

Ten snares seemed like overkill. The very first would likely catch the first groping or trailing foot – the loop would tighten – the murderer would kick and thrash and fail to break away, but the other foot would probably foul another loop, and tighten it, so that both feet were caught, which was a good reason for having more than one snare. It was possible that by some crazy luck (pheasants had this luck occasionally) the murderer would clear two and three and four snares without falling into a loop. Not ten.

The murderer would come. The murderer would be snared. The murderer would, by the fact of coming, say, 'I killed Piet Vandervelde' in a voice bearing total conviction.

Total conviction, thought Dan, pleased with the pun.

He realized he was terribly tired – too tired. He desperately wanted sleep. His internal clock was practically guaranteed to wake him up to orders, but it had let him down once already in the last mad seventy-two hours. Cedric had come on him then, but it would not be Cedric in the dawn. He could not take the risk. Tired as he was he must stay awake.

He became aware how cold he was, his coat being Cedric's mattress. Being cold would keep him awake, which was good. It might make his fingers numb, which was probably bad; but it might not matter, because he might not need his fingers, or have any chance to use them; he might not have any need for them ever again.

He went back to the hut. Out of the blackness inside the gaping door he heard Cedric's untroubled breathing. It was the breathing of somebody who trusted the person she was with. It made another reason to stay awake.

Dan sat in the door of the hut, his arms round his knees. He clenched his teeth to stop them chattering with cold. The night was very still. Cedric's breathing, a fathom away in the darkness behind him, was like the bellows of elfland faintly blowing.

Dan was sure that, unless a tempest came up, he would hear the murderer coming from a long way off in the wood. Then he would move, like a spider, to his hiding place beside the path, beside the snares.

The very first and faintest pallor entered the sky over the dark tangle of the river-woods, to the east.

There was no sound. No tempest blew up. No murderer was yet crunching and squelching through the woods towards the footbridge.

Reluctantly, Dan woke Cedric. It was still pitch-dark in the hut. Cedric saw no merit in waking, and was not yet interested in breakfast. Dan dared not let her sleep. He sat her beside him in the door of the hut, wrapped in both his coats. The sky grew ever so slightly paler. Dan listened intently for feet on wet ground, for breaking twigs, on the other side of the river.

'Now that I can see to shoot,' said a voice, 'I'm going to do it.'

The murderer was sitting on the ground six yards from the hut, with a twelve-bore shotgun pointing at Dan and Cedric.

11

'Hullo, Uncle Ralph,' said Cedric.

Ralph Watts was wearing a fleece-padded anorak with a hood, shooting gloves, and fur-lined boots. He was warm. His fingers were not numb and his hands would not tremble.

His right hand held the gun steady on his knees as his left pushed back the hood. He was as small and gingery as Dan remembered. He was in the greatest imaginable contrast to the man Cedric had described: the diametrically opposite man.

Ralph Watts had both hands on the gun now, and he was pointing it at Dan's chest. He said, 'I know you thought I thought Anna was with some women. But Anna told Sylvia she was with you.'

'Is that true?' Dan asked Cedric, extremely startled.

'Yes, of course,' said Cedric, who did not seem to have taken in the horror of the present situation. 'I knew Mummy wouldn't worry about me if she knew I was with you. She wouldn't have hundreds of policemen searching for me and spoiling everything.'

'That's about right,' said Ralph Watts pleasantly. 'Great tribute, Mallett. Sylvia trusts you. Still has more of a soft spot for you than I quite like – another reason for this morning's operation. Not the important one, but an extra one. I don't want my millionairess bride having soft spots for old flames. It doesn't make for emotional tranquillity or economic security. Anyway, Sylvia knew you thought *she* thought Anna was with those females the child invented, away in Leicestershire or somewhere. Sylvia thought it was a good idea, having Anna safely out of the place while a murder investigation was going on. No place for an impressionable child, Sylvia thought. So she was grateful to you. I was too, for different reasons. Sylvia thought Anna would have a lot of fun with you, and learn a lot. I expect she did learn a lot. Pity it's all going to be wasted.'

Yes, pity, thought Dan.

'I knew enough about you, from Sylvia and people in the village, to know what to expect here this morning,' said Ralph Watts. 'Nets or booby-traps or something. But I had to come, after getting that telephone message. So I borrowed Sylvia's rubber dinghy. I don't know why you thought I'd have to come over that grotty bridge.'

A sense of his folly hit Dan like a sandbag. It had never occurred to him to use a boat to get to this or any other part of the river. He had never had the use of a boat. He had hardly any experience of boats. You were conspicuous in a boat, visible, helpless; and Dan hated being conspicuous. He was one for crawling through sedges at the edge of a river, not lording it in front of the world in the middle. Boats had simply not come into his reckoning.

As soon as he got the telephone call from Julie's friend in Liverpool, Ralph Watts must have got hold of the boat. And probably of a large-scale map, a six-inch-to-the-mile Ordnance Survey. He was an estate agent, and would know about maps and judging distances and compass bearings. He was a country-man, who saw where to go and how to get there. He had probably started immediately after that, going downstream in the boat. He knew he'd get to the island long before Dan did. He sat comfortable and warm, watching them arrive, watching Dan lay his snares and pat himself on the back. Content to wait until it was light enough to shoot.

Noise of the gun? No problem. Early morning duck shooting.

Nobody would ever find the bodies, because nobody would ever think to look for them. Dan and Cedric would simply have disappeared, together or separately, at the other end of the county or in some other county. Nobody would know she had ever looked like a boy. Nobody who had seen Cedric would connect that audacious boy with sticking-out ears with the missing little girl.

Dan had dug a pit, and Dan had walked into it. Dan had

baited the hook, and Dan had swallowed the hook. He had used live bait, and soon it would be dead bait.

'Can you satisfy my curiosity,' said Dan, 'as a kind of last favour?'

'Sure, if it doesn't take long.'

'You got the message to Piet Vandervelde that Anna was going to be at home, and Sylvia wasn't and the dog wasn't, knowing that would bring him?'

Cedric blinked at her father's name. She did not otherwise visibly react.

'Yes, of course,' said Ralph Watts. 'As I told the police. I thought I'd better do that before they found out for themselves. I was one of only about five people who knew about Sylvia and the dog. I thought it would bring the bastard.'

'Were you going to try to talk to him?'

'I wasn't even going to let him see me, if I could help it.'

'But he did see you. You had some sort of fight.'

'Yes, he tried to take the gun away from me. I was against that.'

'I can see you might be . . . Why did you say you'd been anywhere near the place?'

'I wouldn't have done, but I thought I'd been spotted. Fellow looked me full in the face, near the house, and could have described me. Would have described me, as soon as someone found the body. So I had to come out and say I'd been there.'

'Blinky Bliss,' said Dan, suddenly remembering. 'My God, what an irony. He didn't have his glasses on. Couldn't have told the parson from a pony.'

'So I found out later,' said Ralph Watts, smiling cheerfully at the irony which he seemed to enjoy more than Dan did. 'I was sitting in my hide-out wondering what the hell to say to the police, when Anna rang me up.'

'Did *what?*' said Dan, completely startled again.

'Yesterday morning,' said Cedric, 'outside the post office. Before we went to the gallops and I rode Quintus. I rang up Uncle Ralph at his special secret number. Mummy had lost it because I had it.'

'*That's* who you were talking to,' said Dan, remembering

Cedric's earnestness in the telephone-box, her refusal to be hurried or interrupted.

'That's who she was talking to,' said Ralph Watts comfortably.

'Lucinda Hanbury's not really a friend of mine at all,' said Cedric. 'And they would never have gone to get her out of prayers. But it's quite true that my guinea-pigs are called Nicholas and Tiggy.'

'Nugget o' truth,' said Dan. 'Right reassuring.'

'Anna told me what she'd told you and the bobby's daughter,' said Ralph Watts. 'She told me how she'd described the fat man. The bobby's daughter had obviously told the other bobbies, so it seemed to me highly desirable to have that description confirmed. A cross-bearing, as you might say. Evidence of another pair of eyes. Everybody thereafter agog to find a big fat character with a black beard. And always will be.'

'Even so, you might have been better with an alibi for Saturday night,' said Dan. 'Pretending you'd never been near the Old Hall.'

'I had an alibi fixed up,' said Ralph Watts. 'Didn't want to use it unless I had to, owing to subsequent problems at an emotional level.'

'A girl,' said Dan.

'Stretching a point. She works behind the bar in a roadhouse near my hide-out.'

'Where is this mysterious hide-out?'

'Bedsit over the garage of the roadhouse, midway between here and home. Simply a place to escape to, with a bird or alone.' ·

'I don't get it,' said Dan.

'You would if you lived with my mother and sister and three dozen bloody dogs. However, I shall shortly be moving to more congenial quarters, with only *one* dog. I may abandon my bolt-hole. Needless extravagance. Not that I shall ever have to worry about *that* again.'

'Who stole the silver?' said Dan, remembering another oddity, and quite anxious to prolong the conversation until he had thought of a way of saving both their lives.

'I did, of course,' said Cedric.

'Ah,' said Dan.

'It wasn't really stealing, not like you do. It was mine anyway. Sort of mine. It was only a few candlesticks and things, off the sideboard in the dining-room. I hid them in the garage, where there's a hollow wall with a hole in it. I often hide things there.'

'What was the point of that?' asked Dan.

'So people would think the big fat man with a boil was a burglar, of course,' said Cedric.

'Of course,' said Dan humbly. 'I suppose it was you who phoned the police, too? Straightaway, before Julie had a chance to? Telephoned,' he corrected himself, seeing the look in Cedric's eye.

'Yes. I'd never dialled 999, and I've always wanted to. I thought it was my *duty*.'

'You put on one of your voices.'

'I did be talken a sight common,' said Cedric. She giggled. It was still a cheerful reunion to her. She saw nothing threatening about the shotgun. She was a country child, used to seeing people with guns, especially in the autumn. A man like Ralph Watts, in November, would look naked without either a shotgun or a riding-whip.

Cedric said, 'There's another thing I expect you're wondering.'

'A few,' said Dan.

'Well, I expect you're wondering why the police didn't find your fingerprints in the car we borrowed after the races, and find out they were yours, and send a message on the radio to the policemen who gave us a lift.'

'I did wonder about that,' said Dan.

'Well, I stayed behind in the car for a bit, after you started off walking to the garage.'

Dan pondered, remembered that this was so, and then hit his head with the flat of his hand in astounded admiration.

'You wiped off the fingerprints before you joined me,' he said.

'It did seem a good idea.'

'It was a good idea.'

149

'It was a good thing I made you come with me on Saturday night.'

'Some advantages,' said Dan. 'Bonus points.'

The daylight was strengthening. Beyond Ralph Watts, Dan could now see the rubber dinghy pulled out of the river on to the bank. Two oars lay in it, neatly crossed like a spoon and fork on a plate. A simple, familiar, commonplace object, which he had left totally and fatally out of his calculations.

It was a morning of miraculous peace. There was a hazy veil of mist over marshes and water-meadows, and the trees of the river-woods loomed shaggy and friendly. Larks were singing, close to the ground instead of spiralling skywards. A robin was singing in the woods, his hard little voice coming clearly over the smooth water. A thrush joined him. A dabchick plopped into a dive, leaving a ring on the water like that of a rising trout.

'I'm hungry,' said Cedric.

She was bundled in Dan's tweed coat, over his banker's coat, over her own disgraceful clothes. Dan glanced at Ralph Watts, wondering if his heart was touched. It seemed not. It seemed he continued determined to have Sylvia and all her money and all Piet Vandervelde's money which would otherwise one day be Cedric's. He was not touched by Cedric's youth or vulnerability, or by her incongruous garments. But he might be hungry. He might be thirsty. He had been sitting on the island for about eight hours.

'Condemned man ate a hearty breakfast,' said Dan. 'Any objections?'

'I heard something clink when you arrived,' said Ralph Watts, as though discussing the weather or local wildlife. 'What was it? Tinned food? Beer?'

'Pepsi-Cola,' said Cedric. 'Do you want some, Uncle Ralph?'

Without moving from the step of the hut, covered continually by the shotgun, Dan leaned inside. He pulled half a dozen cans of Pepsi and the bag of sausage rolls towards the door.

Cedric's hunger had given Dan an idea. A thin chance but their only one.

Nearly all the girls Dan had ever known were incapable of throwing: they bent their arms wrong. Things they threw went off at right angles. Dan thought Cedric might be an exception, being an exception in every other way.

'We can spare a couple,' Dan said to Ralph Watts. 'Final picnic. No hard feelings. You'd like us to stay where we are, I imagine?'

'Yes,' said Ralph Watts.

Dan also wanted Cedric and himself to stay where they were, for the moment, because of what came next.

'Chuck your Uncle Ralph a couple of cans,' said Dan to Cedric. 'Chuck them together.'

'Not one by one?' said Cedric, puzzled.

'Together,' said Dan.

Ralph Watts sat quiet, alert. He was taking in what was going on without, Dan thought, taking in quite all of it. He did not seem to understand, any more than Cedric understood, the reason Dan wanted the two cans of Pepsi tossed across the ground simultaneously.

Cedric picked up two cans. She held one in each hand.

'Put 'em together,' said Dan. 'Chuck 'em like this.'

He demonstrated the two-handed action of a basketball player.

Puzzled but trusting (or uncharacteristically obedient) Cedric clinked the cans together in her two small hands. She cradled them against her chest.

Dan tried to look as though he were sitting absolutely relaxed, resigned. He was not holding a can or anything else. His hands were on his knees, palms up, empty. It was almost a gesture of surrender, of helplessness. He did not want to use a can as a missile. He did not want Ralph Watts to think he was planning to throw a can or the bag of sausage rolls or one of his shoes. He wanted Ralph Watts to be thinking, unworriedly, about the cans of Pepsi Cedric was about to toss him.

'Get on, then,' said Dan mildly to Cedric. 'Your Uncle Ralph must be dying of thirst.'

'I think *we* need them all,' said Cedric. 'We're dying of thirst. He should have brought his own.'

'That's selfish,' said Dan. 'You should always share with those less fortunate.'

'Oh, all right,' said Cedric.

She lobbed the two cans, quite high, pushing them away from her chest as though they were a single basketball, following Dan's demonstration. They curved upwards, almost together. Dan had been right. Cedric's throw was entirely competent. The cans were about a foot apart at the top of their parabola, a little over half-way between Cedric and Ralph Watts. As they fell towards him, they drifted a few more inches apart. They seemed to travel lazily, unnaturally slowly.

Dan's theory was that if you threw two things at a man – things that he wanted – he was apt to try to catch them both. Ralph Watts could have let both cans fall, on his lap or on the ground beside him. They would have come to no harm, would not have burst, nor the fizz have become too explosive. Or he could have caught one, whichever went to his left hand, and let the other fall where it fell. But Dan was banking on an instinct that Ralph Watts, instinctively, would drop whatever he was holding in order to field both cans.

Ralph Watts dropped the shotgun in his lap, and grabbed for both cans.

Even as they slapped on to his open palms, Dan was on him. He seemed to himself to have covered the ground in a dive, not touching the ground. This was clearly not so, but he moved very fast indeed. There was a split second during which Ralph Watts's eyes were on the cans and his hands were spread waiting for the cans and his gun was in his lap. It was that split second which Dan occupied with crossing the ground and landing on him. Dan and the Pepsi-Cola, almost together. Dan used a straight-arm to Ralph Watts's eye and with his other hand grabbed for the gun.

Ralph Watts had the gun again. They rolled over and over, the gun between them. It was a wildcat fight. They were evenly matched. Ralph Watts was as hard and fit as Dan was, a point-to-point rider, dieting and running and weight-training. Neither let go of the gun or of the other. They rolled one way and then back, in glutinous, stinking mud. They rolled, struggling, into the rubber dinghy, which overturned. The oars tumbled on top of them. They rolled on to one of the oars and broke it. Splinters of wood cut them. The breath of both men rasped. They were bleeding from each other's fingernails and teeth and from the splinters of wood; they were caked in stinking mud.

The gun went off. The noise, between their chests, was terrific. The muzzle of the gun was between their faces, and shot singed Dan's cheek. The full charge crashed into the rubber dinghy. They rolled another way and suddenly they were in the filthy and freezing water. Both were now sobbing with exhaustion, with desperation. They fought like animals, the gun always between them.

Dan's conscious mind was barely working. Every bit of his brain and strength was concentrated on the life-or-death fight. But a bit of his mind guessed that Ralph Watts was a better swimmer than himself. A bit of his mind doubted if the gun would work, its barrels full of muddy water and the remaining cartridge wet.

They were caught in an endless patch of soggy, withered sedge. Flailing legs stirred up the mud, and a new, horrible smell of underwater decay.

Suddenly Ralph Watts let go of the useless gun and of Dan, and scrambled ashore, grabbing at handfuls of sedge. He squelched on to the bank and broke into a shambling run. Dan was incapable of following him.

Ignoring Cedric, Ralph Watts stumbled towards the foot-bridge.

It came to Dan that last night Ralph had heard the car arrive. He would know from the sound approximately where it had been left. He was taking it.

Almost at the footbridge, first one of his feet and then the other caught in a snare. He had forgotten the snares. Anybody might, after such a battle. Dan himself had forgotten the snares. Ralph Watts's impetus carried him forward, and he landed with a crack on the end of the log which made the footbridge.

Dan, holding the gun, found himself incapable of bearing its weight. He dropped it. It disappeared into the black water.

Cedric helped Dan ashore. He needed help. He collapsed on the bank, a mud man, dripping and stinking and bleeding and fighting for breath. He thought no part of him was broken, but none was undamaged.

'Is Uncle Ralph dead?' asked Cedric presently.

'Doubt it,' said Dan, with difficulty.

He walked with difficulty, too, to the end of the footbridge, avoiding the other eight snares. Ralph Watts was not dead, and would not long be unconscious. Dan tied his wrists and ankles with the nylon of two of the snares. They embarked on the business of getting him to the car.

Sylvia stared at the two of them, speechlessly, as they got out of the car. Dan had great difficulty in straightening and standing. He was still coated in mud, his face a mask of mud and blood.

Cedric was a sharp-faced little boy, unusually short-haired for his age, with sticking-out ears.

'Passenger's about like me,' said Dan.

Sylvia screamed when she saw Ralph Watts, half conscious, half dead, stretched across the back seat of the car.

Dan, bathed and disinfected and patched up and dressed in clean clothes, sat in the drawing-room of Medwell Old Hall with Sylvia and the Detective Chief Superintendent.

Anna came in, dressed as a girl. Sylvia sent her out again. As she went through the door Dan called to her, 'Where did you get the name Terry Corbett?'

'Cedric Maltravers' best chum,' said Anna. 'On HMS *Clarion* in the China Station.'

Anna disappeared.

'Amazen,' said Dan, reminding himself to adopt a modified yokel voice for the Superintendent. There was no call to show the bluebottles that he could be a bank-manager, or a Captain of Marines. 'Bloke wi' a belly an' a beard an' a boil an' even a name.'

'The child completely invented the description!' said the Superintendent slowly, like a man emerging from shock. 'And she had you believing it, and at one remove the police forces of the entire British Isles believing it. What made you realize there wasn't any such person?'

'I were a mite slow,' said Dan. 'Cam t'me that every place thicky bloke were at, were a place Cedric . . . were a place Anna wanted t'go, but her Mam niver let her. See, like 'at breakfast in bed. Niver allowed at home, an' she did long for t'gobble in bed. *So*, off we goes t'Stepleton. She said she saw bloke in a shop. A-b'lieved un, a-course a-b'lieved un. But 'twere all for breakfast in bed. Never were no such bloke t'Stepleton. Then it were the races. Longed t'go racen, she did, but her Mam niver let her. So she had the bloke a-riden by on a bike, wi' race-glasses a-danglen from his shouldy. Very clever, I were, putten two an' two together 'at tide, an' maken out the bloke were goen racen.'

'Go on,' said Sylvia faintly.

'Then she seed un, she say, a-hoppen into a harse-box. So off we goes t'trainen-stable. Summat she wanted t'see, 'at's all. Then they gallops. She did get t'sit a harse. Kindly blokes, seemenly. They niver *did* gi' nobody no lift. She made it all up, see, so's t'go t'stable an' gallops. Swimmen-bath nex', an' fish'an'-chips. Halloween doens in school-house. Boilerman, she said he were. Still a-b'lieved un. Why not? Big, black Terry Corbett, wi' belly an' beard an' boil. Mebbe a-might ha' had doubts, ay, a-b'lieves a-might, but for one thing. Heard tell Ralph Watts did see the same bloke, jus' hereabouts, night o' the killen.'

'And in describing the imaginary man he said he saw,' said the Superintendent, 'Ralph Watts was simply quoting Anna's description of the imaginary man *she* said *she* saw. A description which she gave him on the telephone.'

'Ay. An' then it cam t'me in boiler-place, a-ben chasen a shadow.'

'A shadow who was in all respects the precise opposite of Watts,' said the Superintendent. 'Hence each detail of the description. The boil was a good touch, extremely convincing. Gave us all something specific to look for, and lent total verisimitude.'

'Ar?' said Dan, with yokel puzzlement.

'It sounded true. But why was she at such pains to protect Watts?'

'Acos he pramised her a doggie,' said Dan.

'Yes, that's quite true,' said Sylvia. 'For her next birthday. A Norwich terrier, he said.'

''At's how a-knew it were him she were protecken,' said Dan.

'Him and no other,' said the Superintendent. 'Yes. It was a shrewd guess, but it was only a guess.'

'Ay. 'At's why we did need the marnen's party, for t'prove he were the one.'

'Yes. How did you get him to the island? What was the message? What did you tell Julie Gundry to tell her friend to tell Watts?'

'It were a mite wrapped up. What it cam to were that Cedric . . . that Anna'd changed her mind. 'At was what Muss Watts did hear, t'telephone las' evenen.'

'Simple as that.'

'Ay. A did b'lieve 'twould bring un. Bait on hook, see.'

'Another thing,' said the Superintendent.

'Ar,' said Dan warily, waiting for questions about borrowed cars.

'We know why Anna ran away. But why did you yourself run? You had a complete alibi.'

Dan looked at him, startled. He glanced at Sylvia. She giggled, then quickly looked as serious as a lady should whose husband had been murdered four days previously, and whose suitor was in custody in Milchester prison for the murder.

'Julie Gundry naturally told us, as it was her legal and moral duty to do,' said the Superintendent. 'Not at once, only yesterday. The delay was wrong but understandable. Of course her statement was in the strictest confidence.'

'Her Dad . . .'

'If he ever knows it will be from her, not from us.'

'She's a lucky girl,' said Sylvia, most unexpectedly.

'There were matter o' me bike,' said Dan. 'Covered wi' me fingerprinties, an' leanen bold as brass nex' the door . . .'

'That's exactly why you were never suspected of any criminal intent,' said the Superintendent. 'You weren't even committing trespass, as you were the invited visitor of a legitimate resident of the house. If you had come to burgle, let alone to commit murder . . .'

'I'd ha' hid me bike,' said Dan slowly.

'Of course you would, you cunning little villain.'

'Gum,' said Dan. 'Fancy.'

'Little Anna has now given us a clear and obviously accurate account of the events of Saturday night, including a positive, undoubted identification of the murderer. What changed her mind? Why did she suddenly decide to stop protecting him?'

'I ben wonderen, too,' said Dan. 'Us c'd mebbe ask un.'

'You ask her, Dan,' said Sylvia. 'She'll tell you anything. You're her idol now.'

'Hum,' said Dan, extremely pleased.

'Of course I changed my mind,' said Anna. 'You were there when he said it. When he said what made me change my mind. You were there. Don't you remember?'

'Seems not,' said Dan apologetically.

'He said, "I'm moving to a new house where there'll only be one dog, instead of thirty like at home." He meant my house. *This* house. He was going to come here.'

'Yes. You knew that all along.'

'"And there'll only be *one* dog there," he said. He meant Sophie, Mummy's dog. Only Sophie. No other dog. *He wasn't going to give me a dog, like he promised*.'

'I'll give you a dog,' said Dan.

Anna kissed him.

THE PERENNIAL LIBRARY MYSTERY SERIES

Delano Ames

CORPSE DIPLOMATIQUE   P 637, $2.84
"Sprightly and intelligent."

—*New York Herald Tribune Book Review*

FOR OLD CRIME'S SAKE   P 629, $2.84

MURDER, MAESTRO, PLEASE   P 630, $2.84
"If there is a more engaging couple in modern fiction than Jane and
Dagobert Brown, we have not met them."   —*Scotsman*

SHE SHALL HAVE MURDER   P 638, $2.84
"Combines the merit of both the English and American schools in the
new mystery. It's as breezy as the best of the American ones, and has
the sophistication and wit of any top-notch Britisher."

—*New York Herald Tribune Book Review*

E. C. Bentley

TRENT'S LAST CASE   P̌ 440, $2.50
"One of the three best detective stories ever written."

—Agatha Christie

TRENT'S OWN CASE   P 516, $2.25
"I won't waste time saying that the plot is sound and the detection
satisfying. Trent has not altered a scrap and reappears with all his old
humor and charm."   —Dorothy L. Sayers

Gavin Black

A DRAGON FOR CHRISTMAS   P 473, $1.95
"Potent excitement!"   —*New York Herald Tribune*

THE EYES AROUND ME   P 485, $1.95
"I stayed up until all hours last night reading *The Eyes Around Me,*
which is something I do not do very often, but I was so intrigued by the
ingeniousness of Mr. Black's plotting and the witty way in which he spins
his mystery. I can only say that I enjoyed the book enormously."

—F. van Wyck Mason

YOU WANT TO DIE, JOHNNY?   P 472, $1.95
"Gavin Black doesn't just develop a pressure plot in suspense, he adds
uninfected wit, character, charm, and sharp knowledge of the Far East
to make rereading as keen as the first race-through."   —*Book Week*

THOU SHELL OF DEATH P 428, $1.95

"It has all the virtues of culture, intelligence and sensibility that the most exacting connoisseur could ask of detective fiction."

—*The Times* [London] *Literary Supplement*

THE WIDOW'S CRUISE P 399, $2.25

"A stirring suspense. . . . The thrilling tale leaves nothing to be desired."

—*Springfield Republican*

THE WORM OF DEATH P 400, $2.25

"It [The Worm of Death] is one of Blake's very best—and his best is better than almost anyone's." —Louis Untermeyer

John & Emery Bonett

A BANNER FOR PEGASUS P 554, $2.40

"A gem! Beautifully plotted and set. . . . Not only is the murder adroit and deserved, and the detection competent, but the love story is charming." —Jacques Barzun and Wendell Hertig Taylor

DEAD LION P 563, $2.40

"A clever plot, authentic background and interesting characters highly recommended this one." —*New Republic*

Christianna Brand

GREEN FOR DANGER P 551, $2.50

"You have to reach for the greatest of Great Names (Christie, Carr, Queen . . .) to find Brand's rivals in the devious subtleties of the trade."

—Anthony Boucher

TOUR DE FORCE P 572, $2.40

"Complete with traps for the over-ingenious, a double-reverse surprise ending and a key clue planted so fairly and obviously that you completely overlook it. If that's your idea of perfect entertainment, then seize at once upon *Tour de Force.*" —Anthony Boucher, *The New York Times*

James Byrom

OR BE HE DEAD P 585, $2.84

"A very original tale . . . Well written and steadily entertaining."

—Jacques Barzun & Wendell Hertig Taylor, *A Catalogue of Crime*

Henry Calvin

IT'S DIFFERENT ABROAD P 640, $2.84

"What is remarkable and delightful, Mr. Calvin imparts a flavor of satire to what he renovates and compels us to take straight."

—Jacques Barzun

Marjorie Carleton

VANISHED P 559, $2.40

"Exceptional . . . a minor triumph."

—Jacques Barzun and Wendell Hertig Taylor, *A Catalogue of Crime*

George Harmon Coxe

MURDER WITH PICTURES P 527, $2.25

"[Coxe] has hit the bull's-eye with his first shot."

—*The New York Times*

Edmund Crispin

BURIED FOR PLEASURE P 506, $2.50

"Absolute and unalloyed delight."

—Anthony Boucher, *The New York Times*

Lionel Davidson

THE MENORAH MEN P 592, $2.84

"Of his fellow thriller writers, only John Le Carré shows the same instinct for the viscera." —*Chicago Tribune*

NIGHT OF WENCESLAS P 595, $2.84

"A most ingenious thriller, so enriched with style, wit, and a sense of serious comedy that it all but transcends its kind."

—*The New Yorker*

THE ROSE OF TIBET P 593, $2.84

"I hadn't realized how much I missed the genuine Adventure story . . . until I read *The Rose of Tibet*." —Graham Greene

D. M. Devine

MY BROTHER'S KILLER P 558, $2.40

"A most enjoyable crime story which I enjoyed reading down to the last moment." —Agatha Christie

Kenneth Fearing

THE BIG CLOCK   P 500, $1.95

"It will be some time before chill-hungry clients meet again so rare a compound of irony, satire, and icy-fingered narrative. *The Big Clock* is . . . a psychothriller you won't put down."   —*Weekly Book Review*

Andrew Garve

THE ASHES OF LODA   P 430, $1.50

"Garve . . . embellishes a fine fast adventure story with a more credible picture of the U.S.S.R. than is offered in most thrillers."

                    —*The New York Times Book Review*

THE CUCKOO LINE AFFAIR   P 451, $1.95

". . . an agreeable and ingenious piece of work."   —*The New Yorker*

A HERO FOR LEANDA   P 429, $1.50

"One can trust Mr. Garve to put a fresh twist to any situation, and the ending is really a lovely surprise."   —*The Manchester Guardian*

MURDER THROUGH THE LOOKING GLASS   P 449, $1.95

". . . refreshingly out-of-the-way and enjoyable . . . highly recommended to all comers."   —*Saturday Review*

NO TEARS FOR HILDA   P 441, $1.95

"It starts fine and finishes finer. I got behind on breathing watching Max get not only his man but his woman, too."   —Rex Stout

THE RIDDLE OF SAMSON   P 450, $1.95

"The story is an excellent one, the people are quite likable, and the writing is superior."   —*Springfield Republican*

Michael Gilbert

BLOOD AND JUDGMENT   P 446, $1.95

"Gilbert readers need scarcely be told that the characters all come alive at first sight, and that his surpassing talent for narration enhances any plot. . . . Don't miss."   —*San Francisco Chronicle*

THE BODY OF A GIRL   P 459, $1.95

"Does what a good mystery should do: open up into all kinds of ramifications, with untold menace behind the action. At the end, there is a bang-up climax, and it is a pleasure to see how skilfully Gilbert wraps everything up."   —*The New York Times Book Review*

Michael Gilbert (cont'd)

THE DANGER WITHIN   P 448, $1.95
"Michael Gilbert has nicely combined some elements of the straight
detective story with plenty of action, suspense, and adventure, to pro-
duce a superior thriller."   —*Saturday Review*

FEAR TO TREAD   P 458, $1.95
"Merits serious consideration as a work of art."
                                     —*The New York Times*

Joe Gores

HAMMETT   P 631, $2.84
"Joe Gores at his very best. Terse, powerful writing—with the master,
Dashiell Hammett, as the protagonist in a novel I think he would have
been proud to call his own."   —Robert Ludlum

C. W. Grafton

BEYOND A REASONABLE DOUBT   P 519, $1.95
"A very ingenious tale of murder . . . a brilliant and gripping narrative."
                                     —Jacques Barzun and Wendell Hertig Taylor

THE RAT BEGAN TO GNAW THE ROPE   P 639, $2.84
"Fast, humorous story with flashes of brilliance."
                                     —*The New Yorker*

Edward Grierson

THE SECOND MAN   P 528, $2.25
"One of the best trial-testimony books to have come along in quite a
while."   —*The New Yorker*

Bruce Hamilton

TOO MUCH OF WATER   P 635, $2.84
"A superb sea mystery. . . . The prose is excellent."
                     —Jacques Barzun and Wendell Hertig Taylor, *A Catalogue of Crime*

Cyril Hare

DEATH IS NO SPORTSMAN   P 555, $2.40
"You will be thrilled because it succeeds in placing an ingenious story
in a new and refreshing setting. . . . The identity of the murderer is really
a surprise."   —*Daily Mirror*

DEATH WALKS THE WOODS P 556, $2.40

"Here is a fine formal detective story, with a technically brilliant solution demanding the attention of all connoisseurs of construction."

—Anthony Boucher, *The New York Times Book Review*

AN ENGLISH MURDER P 455, $2.50

"By a long shot, the best crime story I have read for a long time. Everything is traditional, but originality does not suffer. The setting is perfect. Full marks to Mr. Hare." —*Irish Press*

SUICIDE EXCEPTED P 636, $2.84

"Adroit in its manipulation . . . and distinguished by a plot-twister which I'll wager Christie wishes she'd thought of."

—*The New York Times*

TENANT FOR DEATH P 570, $2.84

"The way in which an air of probability is combined both with clear, terse narrative and with a good deal of subtle suburban atmosphere, proves the extreme skill of the writer." —*The Spectator*

TRAGEDY AT LAW P 522, $2.25

"An extremely urbane and well-written detective story."

—*The New York Times*

UNTIMELY DEATH P 514, $2.25

"The English detective story at its quiet best, meticulously underplayed, rich in perceivings of the droll human animal and ready at the last with a neat surprise which has been there all the while had we but wits to see it." —*New York Herald Tribune Book Review*

THE WIND BLOWS DEATH P 589, $2.84

"A plot compounded of musical knowledge, a Dickens allusion, and a subtle point in law is related with delightfully unobtrusive wit, warmth, and style." —*The New York Times*

WITH A BARE BODKIN P 523, $2.25

"One of the best detective stories published for a long time."

—*The Spectator*

Robert Harling

THE ENORMOUS SHADOW P 545, $2.50

"In some ways the best spy story of the modern period. . . . The writing is terse and vivid . . . the ending full of action . . . altogether first-rate."

—Jacques Barzun and Wendell Hertig Taylor, *A Catalogue of Crime*

Francis Iles

BEFORE THE FACT   P 517, $2.50
"Not many 'serious' novelists have produced character studies to compare with Iles's internally terrifying portrait of the murderer in *Before the Fact,* his masterpiece and a work truly deserving the appellation of unique and beyond price."   —Howard Haycraft

MALICE AFORETHOUGHT   P 532, $1.95
"It is a long time since I have read anything so good as *Malice Afore-thought,* with its cynical humour, acute criminology, plausible detail and rapid movement. It makes you hug yourself with pleasure."
      —H. C. Harwood, *Saturday Review*

Michael Innes

THE CASE OF THE JOURNEYING BOY   P 632, $3.12
"I could see no faults in it. There is no one to compare with him."
      —*Illustrated London News*

DEATH BY WATER   P 574, $2.40
"The amount of ironic social criticism and deft characterization of scenes and people would serve another author for six books."
      —Jacques Barzun and Wendell Hertig Taylor

HARE SITTING UP   P 590, $2.84
"There is hardly anyone (in mysteries or mainstream) more exquisitely literate, allusive and Jamesian—and hardly anyone with a firmer sense of melodramatic plot or a more vigorous gift of storytelling."
      —Anthony Boucher, *The New York Times*

THE LONG FAREWELL   P 575, $2.40
"A model of the deft, classic detective story, told in the most wittily diverting prose."   —*The New York Times*

THE MAN FROM THE SEA   P 591, $2.84
"The pace is brisk, the adventures exciting and excitingly told, and above all he keeps to the very end the interesting ambiguity of the man from the sea."   —*New Statesman*

THE SECRET VANGUARD   P 584, $2.84
"Innes . . . has mastered the art of swift, exciting and well-organized narrative."   —*The New York Times*

THE WEIGHT OF THE EVIDENCE   P 633, $2.84
"First-class puzzle, deftly solved. University background interesting and amusing."   —*Saturday Review of Literature*

Mary Kelly

THE SPOILT KILL P 565, $2.40

"Mary Kelly is a new Dorothy Sayers. . . . [An] exciting new novel."
—*Evening News*

Lange Lewis

THE BIRTHDAY MURDER P 518, $1.95

"Almost perfect in its playlike purity and delightful prose."
—Jacques Barzun and Wendell Hertig Taylor

Allan MacKinnon

HOUSE OF DARKNESS P 582, $2.84

"His best . . . a perfect compendium."
—Jacques Barzun & Wendell Hertig Taylor, *A Catalogue of Crime*

Arthur Maling

LUCKY DEVIL P 482, $1.95

"The plot unravels at a fast clip, the writing is breezy and Maling's approach is as fresh as today's stockmarket quotes."
—*Louisville Courier Journal*

RIPOFF P 483, $1.95

"A swiftly paced story of today's big business is larded with intrigue as a Ralph Nader-type investigates an insurance scandal and is soon on the run from a hired gun and his brother. . . . Engrossing and credible."
—*Booklist*

SCHROEDER'S GAME P 484, $1.95

"As the title indicates, this Schroeder is up to something, and the unravelling of his game is a diverting and sufficiently blood-soaked entertainment."
—*The New Yorker*

Austin Ripley

MINUTE MYSTERIES P 387, $2.50

More than one hundred of the world's shortest detective stories. Only one possible solution to each case!

Thomas Sterling

THE EVIL OF THE DAY P 529, $2.50

"Prose as witty and subtle as it is sharp and clear. . .characters unconventionally conceived and richly bodied forth . . . . In short, a novel to be treasured."
—Anthony Boucher, *The New York Times*

Julian Symons

THE BELTING INHERITANCE P 468, $1.95
"A superb whodunit in the best tradition of the detective story."
— August Derleth, *Madison Capital Times*

BLAND BEGINNING P 469, $1.95
"Mr. Symons displays a deft storytelling skill, a quiet and literate wit, a nice feeling for character, and detectival ingenuity of a high order."
— Anthony Boucher, *The New York Times*

BOGUE'S FORTUNE P 481, $1.95
"There's a touch of the old sardonic humour, and more than a touch of style." — *The Spectator*

THE BROKEN PENNY P 480, $1.95
"The most exciting, astonishing and believable spy story to appear in years. — Anthony Boucher, *The New York Times Book Review*

THE COLOR OF MURDER P 461, $1.95
"A singularly unostentatious and memorably brilliant detective story."
— *New York Herald Tribune Book Review*

Dorothy Stockbridge Tillet
(John Stephen Strange)

THE MAN WHO KILLED FORTESCUE P 536, $2.25
"Better than average." — *Saturday Review of Literature*

Simon Troy

THE ROAD TO RHUINE P 583, $2.84
"Unusual and agreeably told." — *San Francisco Chronicle*

SWIFT TO ITS CLOSE P 546, $2.40
"A nicely literate British mystery . . . the atmosphere and the plot are exceptionally well wrought, the dialogue excellent." — *Best Sellers*

Henry Wade

THE DUKE OF YORK'S STEPS P 588, $2.84
"A classic of the golden age."
— Jacques Barzun & Wendell Hertig Taylor, *A Catalogue of Crime*

A DYING FALL P 543, $2.50
"One of those expert British suspense jobs . . . it crackles with undercurrents of blackmail, violent passion and murder. Topnotch in its class."
— *Time*

If you enjoyed this book you'll want to know about THE PERENNIAL LIBRARY MYSTERY SERIES

Buy them at your local bookstore or use this coupon for ordering:

Qty	P number	Price
————	————	————
————	————	————
————	————	————
————	————	————
————	————	————
————	————	————
————	————	————
————	————	————
————	————	————
————	————	————
————	————	————
————	————	————

postage and handling charge $1.00
———— book(s) @ $0.25   ————

TOTAL   ⬚

Prices contained in this coupon are Harper & Row invoice prices only. They are subject to change without notice, and in no way reflect the prices at which these books may be sold by other suppliers.

HARPER & ROW, Mail Order Dept. #PMS, 10 East 53rd St., New York, N.Y. 10022.

Please send me the books I have checked above. I am enclosing $———— which includes a postage and handling charge of $1.00 for the first book and 25¢ for each additional book. Send check or money order. No cash or C.O.D.s please

Name————————————————————————

Address——————————————————————

City———————— State———————— Zip————————

Please allow 4 weeks for delivery. USA only. This offer expires 4/30/85
Please add applicable sales tax.